THE DESTINY GUN

Arc I, Volume I

Hector L. Bones

The Bones Family

Library of Congress Control Number:

Book Cover by Hector L. Bones

Illustrations by Hector L. Bones

1st edition 2025

DEDICATION

*I dedicate this book to my beautiful wife **Debbie N. Bones**, who has been a great support and source of inspiration. She is the most brilliant person I know to which I can count to bounce off ideas and helping me through but also helps me keep on track and complete our projects in life.*

*Without you **Debbie** my love I would never have got the courage to get this book out.*

*I also dedicate this book to my children who inspired me to put my ideas on paper and bring them to life. Thanks **Aerith Nyomi, Alisher Krystal and Aiden Kalel**, for being great kids and an infinite source of inspiration.*

INTRODUCTION

Welcome to Arc I of The Destiny Gun, a story about choice, memory, and the cost of rewriting what the world believes is fixed. This volume opens the larger saga with a simple discovery that refuses to stay small: a young collector, Aiden Cross, stumbles into a mystery—and an inheritance —capable of bending reality's seams.

The object at the heart of this tale is not merely a relic. The Destiny Gun is bound to the planet's ley lines; every use leaves a mark, a change, a ripple that cannot be unfired. The Codex he carries—no ordinary book— remembers, records, and sometimes writes back. That is the first lesson Aiden learns: every shot alters the weave; every choice accrues a cost.

But power is never unobserved. As Aiden and his friends probe deeper, they collide with forces that have long curated history from the shadows. The Order of Destiny tests and threatens; the ledger of past wielders reveals names that do not end so much as vanish—lives struck from remembrance, erased from the page. The discovery is not academic. It is personal. It is a warning.

Across these chapters, the canvas widens—toward Atlantean ruins, sealed corridors, and fractures in what the world believes is fixed. This volume traces the approach to Atlantis rather than its full return: the first cracks in official history, the first hints that Seals are narratives as much as locks, and the realization that someone has been choosing which futures are allowed to exist. From there, the path forks into investigations, field teams, and a race to understand who is writing the world and why. The question that follows Aiden is not whether to act, but whether he can live with the shape of the world his actions leave behind.

At its core, this book is about agency under pressure—about friendships tested in strange light, about guardians who remember more than they should, and about a young man learning that the tightest knots are tied between what we want to save and what we must let go. If you've ever wondered whether history is a fixed text or a living draft, you're in good company here.

With anticipation for the journey ahead,

Hector L. Bones

SYNOPSIS

Arc I, Volume I

Aiden Cross is a collector who can no longer be satisfied by the weight of objects. Coins, watches, postcards—each once a story—have thinned to surface. What he's been reaching for, without words, is the seam where story meets world. He finds it when the Destiny Gun enters his hands, paired with a living Codex that records what should be true and sometimes refuses to accept it. The first time he tests the Gun, the day shivers. A small, undeniable change blooms across the weave of things. The lesson arrives with a quiet chill: every shot is not a projectile but a revision. Every use accrues a cost.

Answers do not come gently. The Gun is bound to the planet's ley lines, and its echo draws watchers. Aiden's circle widens under pressure—a companion attuned to the lines (Blu), a few quick minds with steady hands, and the first shadow of a man who wears Aiden's face and not his life: Sobacco, a splinter-self birthed by the Gun's refusal to leave clean edges. The splinter does not sneer or cackle; he questions. Which choices are Aiden's, and which were written for him? The question is a mirror Aiden cannot look away from.

The world begins to notice. In a garden nexus where the lines knot like roots, something old and floral stirs. In a convention hall crowded with glass and noise, the weave slips and the modern stage groans under ancient weight—a public calamity framed as "glitch," but it's the Gun asserting that history is not a thing that stays put. The Order of Destiny steps out of rumor and into the light with its iron smile. General Alaric, emblem of a long custodianship, does not threaten so much as warn: history survives because someone tends it. The Codex, they imply, is their ledger too.

Aiden's search widens from curiosity to a hunt. He tracks a pattern of "erased wielders," names that do not end so much as vanish; the ledger reads like a list of lives subtracted from the world to preserve the story that needed telling. The decision to keep going is not heroic. It is stubborn and human. The team follows fractures that behave like clues—misremembered streets, rewritten family lore, dates that slip a day to the left—and find talk of seals. Not locks, exactly. Frames. If the seals fall, what they contain is not released so much as allowed to be remembered.

Water becomes the next teacher. In an aquarium's hushed blue, under the long gaze of creatures older than stone clocks, Aiden meets Captain Cofrezi and hears the name spoken carefully: Atlantis. Not the jape of maps but a city that has been sealed into "story" for so long that the world forgot how to see it. When it returns, it does not erupt from the sea. It stabilizes—choosing a form the present can survive. The Primordial Sect calls it restoration. The Order calls it contamination. The Watchers, who do not intervene and therefore shape outcomes by refusing to touch them, simply take note.

Atlantis reshapes the board. The Gun's ripples become waves; friends strain; trust is tested. Sobacco's presence complicates everything—an unasked-for echo that behaves like conscience and temptation in equal measure. The Codex begins to misbehave, pages shivering, entries smearing, then clearing to reveal possibilities like afterimages. Aiden learns what no custodian wanted him to learn: the seals are narratives. To "break" one is to admit an excluded truth back into the draft. Atlantis's return is not a triumphal crown; it is a proof that the world can be rewritten—and that someone has been rewriting it all along.

Cracks spread. The Order of Destiny fractures under its own doctrine, torn between those who would harden the frame and those who admit that curation long ago became control. The Primordial Sect presses its advantage, arguing for a wholesale restoration of the "original world," regardless of who gets ground under that recovery. The Unseen—entities half rumor, half consequence—probe the new edges for places to push. The seventh seal weakens, and the lines hum like wires under weather.

At the Nexus of Fate, where the city and the ley and the Codex's invisible index intersect, the shape of the choice finally stands upright. Aiden is offered two clean hands: enforce the frame (erase the aberrations, close the seams, keep the world coherent at the cost of its missing truths), or swing the gate wide (restore the excluded in one flood and let the world drown or learn to breathe salt). He refuses the cleanliness of either. The shot he takes is not a correction or a cataclysm but a splice—an act that preserves Atlantis as a stabilized echo rather than a conquering tide, that acknowledges the erased without rewriting every page at once. It is the most dangerous thing he can choose: a living draft.

The price is immediate. The Codex blanks like a held breath—its pages no longer a history to obey but a surface that will record what happens next. The Order splinters for real. The Watchers pay attention. The Primordial Sect smiles like a promise. Sobacco does not die; he steps off the map, leaving behind anomalies that behave like footprints and a warning not to let anyone else write the ending. Blu, shaking with ley line feedback, steadies. Aiden learns what wielders before him were not allowed to keep: he retains memory of what he changed.

Arc I closes without triumphal brass. The city is there—choosing its form. The lines hum—less like a weapon's charge, more like a choir warming to a note. The Gun is still the Gun, but it will not be enough to shoot problems until they look like answers. Aiden has a crew, an enemy that thinks it is a parent, a sect that thinks it is a cure, and a book that has decided to wait and see. The world did not end; it bent. The cost is not paid; it has only been named. And somewhere just outside the frame, a splinter walks with Aiden's shadow and a fragment of what the Gun could become. The draft is alive. The next line is theirs to write.

PROLOGUE

The page takes ink, then pushes it back. The page is not telling a tale; it is logging proof.

Name: —

Date: —

Witness: —

Letters appear where no hand moves: Every shot is a revision. The words tremble, decide to stay. Margins gather a map that isn't supposed to exist—narrow streets that turn at a lighthouse no chart remembers. A second hand ticks, then chooses a different second. Tonight, on a narrow desk under a salt-wet pane, where lighthouse fog presses glass. A girl glances left instead of right. Behind her, a bell misses its ring; a meeting never happens. Somewhere, a door unlatches on a day that never had a visitor.

The Codex smells faintly of rain and copper. It keeps verdicts; it does not give orders. The ley lines hum through the spine like wire in winter walls. They conduct the change; something else decides it. Because the shot is unmade, its heat still prints the page.

Another sentence writes itself and erases mid-stroke. Another tries again and fades. A third survives long enough to be read: Designation: Wielder. (Name removed.) Status: not deceased, not alive—omitted. The frost has crossed other names, quick as breath. The strikeout travels across the entry like frost, brittle and fast, until only the pressure of what was there remains —and the air above the page drops three degrees.

The map in the margin darkens. Buildings tilt to make room for a street that wants to exist. Footsteps draw themselves and then pull up, as if the walker remembered they were being watched. Noticed—by eyes that do not belong to ink. In the corner of the page, a shadow divides—one shape, two directions. The ledger stutters—two tracks, one decision left unresolved. One keeps to the light. One walks the edge of the frame and does not mind the edge looking back.

Ink beads, refuses, beads again. The page won't tell a story; it tallies what survives: a smudge in the left margin where a thumb held too tight; a thin scorch that smells like lightning; a ripple in the fibers that behaves like a breath.

A final line writes itself slowly, as if aware it will be weighed: History is a draft. Someone is holding the pen. The page trembles once, as if the pen just lifted.

To the eye, the page is nearly blank. It prefers proofs to stories; so do I. To the hand, the book is heavier when it closes. At first light, we follow the new street the margin insists exists—the one that wasn't there yesterday.

CHAPTER 1: THE ALLURE OF GOLD

A Collector's Restlessness

The early morning sunlight slipped through the cracks in the blinds, casting slanted beams of gold across Aiden's cluttered bedroom. Dust swirled lazily in the air, illuminated by the warm glow, dancing over the endless collection of trinkets and treasures that filled every available space. He wasn't chasing gold anymore; he was chasing proof something was meant for him.

Shelves lined the walls, overflowing with coins from distant lands, medals polished to a perfect shine, and figurines plated in gold. A miniature ship, its delicate hull layered with thin sheets of gold leaf, rested on the highest shelf, glimmering like a relic from a long-forgotten legend. An ornate compass, its needle rusted but its frame untouched by time, lay on his nightstand, beside a stack of yellowed parchment maps. Even his dresser drawers, meant for clothes, had long since become storage for artifacts—a place where old, gilded lockets and bronze-plated watches tangled together.

Aiden sat cross-legged on his bed, absently rolling a golden pendant between his fingers. It was small, circular, and intricately carved with the image of a phoenix mid-flight, its wings curling like flames. He traced the etching with his thumb, feeling the smooth grooves worn down by time.

It wasn't enough. None of it was.

He glanced around his room, once a sanctuary, now a museum of things that had lost their meaning. The shimmering reflections of polished gold no longer stirred excitement in him. His collection had grown too large, too meaningless—each new trinket brought temporary satisfaction, but the moment it joined the others, it became just another lifeless relic in the ever-growing pile.

Aiden sighed, setting the pendant down beside him with a soft clink.

"What am I even doing?" he muttered to himself, running a hand through his messy hair.

He had spent years searching for treasures, tracking down unique items in flea markets, antique shops, and online auctions. He had haggled, traded, and saved every penny just to get his hands on objects that felt like pieces of history. But now, as he stared at them, he felt an emptiness creeping in—a gnawing sense that they were just objects, not stories. Not what he was truly searching for.

A memory surfaced, unbidden. His grandfather's voice, low and thoughtful, as he placed a worn coin into Aiden's small, eager hands years ago.

"It's not the metal that matters, Aiden. It's the journey."

Aiden had been ten years old then, fascinated by the strange etching on the coin—a swirling pattern around an unblinking eye. His grandfather had smiled knowingly, turning the coin over between his fingers.

"Every object tells a story. The trick is knowing how to listen." Some keep the story; some rewrite it.

At the time, Aiden had simply nodded, tucking the coin into his pocket without a second thought. He had been young, impatient. He didn't care about the story, he had cared that it was gold, that it was rare, that it was his.

Now, years later, the words finally sank in, but he had no idea what they truly meant.

Shaking the thought away, he swung his legs over the side of the bed and reached for the morning newspaper lying folded on his desk. It was an old habit—he had always skimmed through the classifieds, just in case something rare or antique caught his eye.

His gaze drifted over the usual sections: local events, politics, sports—until it landed on a tiny, tucked-away ad near the bottom of the page.

"Curiosities and Mysteries – Shop on Crescent Avenue. One-of-a-kind finds for the curious and bold."

Aiden's breath caught.

"Curious and bold." The words felt strangely familiar, as if someone had whispered them to him in a dream.

His heart quickened, a thrill bubbling up from somewhere deep inside him.

Crescent Avenue. That wasn't far—a fifteen-minute bike ride at most. He could call the shop, maybe ask about their inventory, but something held him back. A hesitation. Or maybe… an instinct.

The same instinct that had whispered to him when he had first started collecting treasures. The same restless voice that had always told him: There's something out there. Something more.

Aiden's fingers curled around the edge of the newspaper.

This wasn't just another antique store. He felt it in his bones. First light had sent him here; a street he didn't remember yesterday had turned toward Crescent on its own.

Without another thought, he jumped to his feet, grabbed his jacket, and stuffed the golden pendant into his pocket. He didn't know why he was taking it, but something told him he'd need it.

As he slung his bag over his shoulder and reached for his bike, a fleeting thought crossed his mind:

"Maybe today, I'll find something real."

FLASHBACK: THE LOST KING'S COIN

Aiden gripped the handlebars of his bike as he weaved through the familiar streets of his neighborhood, the morning air crisp against his face. The rhythmic sound of the tires against the pavement did little to quiet his racing thoughts.

Why did that ad feel... different?

He had seen plenty of antique shops before, had spent hours scouring dusty shelves, haggling over prices, and inspecting the fine details of old artifacts. But something about this shop, something about the words "curious and bold"—stirred something deep in him. It was more than a simple curiosity.

It was a pull.

His fingers absentmindedly brushed against the golden phoenix pendant in his jacket pocket, and without meaning to, his mind drifted back to a day long past.

The living room smelled of coffee and old books, the scent mingling with the faint traces of his grandfather's aftershave. Aiden sat cross-legged on the rug, barely able to contain his excitement as his grandfather held out his latest treasure small golden coin that glimmered in the dim light of the old study lamp.

"You see this, Aiden?" his grandfather had said, his voice filled with the quiet reverence he always carried when handling relics.

Aiden, then just ten years old, had reached out eagerly, letting the cool weight of the coin settle in his palm. It was smaller than a quarter, worn smoothly by time, but there was something different about it. Something almost... alive.

"It's gold," Aiden had murmured, running his small fingers over the faint, intricate symbols carved into the surface. "Is it rare?"

His grandfather had chuckled. "More than rare, my boy. This is one of the Lost King's Coins."

Aiden had snapped his head up, eyes wide. "The Lost King? Like the one from the stories?"

The old man nodded. "Indeed. Legends say the Lost King crafted twenty of these coins—not from gold or silver, but from a piece of time itself. They were meant to guide those worthy of his legacy. Some say the coins choose their owners."

The idea had thrilled Aiden back then. A treasure that chooses its wielder? It had sounded like something out of an adventure novel.

"Did it choose you, Grandpa?" he asked.

His grandfather had smiled but said nothing, simply closing Aiden's fingers around the coin. "Every object tells a story, Aiden. The trick is knowing how to listen."

Back in the present, Aiden tightened his grip on his bike handles as the street signs of Crescent Avenue came into view.

He had never forgotten that coin. And even though he had lost it years ago, the words of his grandfather never truly left him.

"Every object tells a story."

Was that why he was here? Not just for another golden artifact, but for a story that actually mattered?

His heart pounded harder, but he wasn't sure if it was from the ride or from something more.

He turned the last corner, and then—

There it was.

A small, unassuming storefront sandwiched between a laundromat and a bakery, its faded gold lettering barely visible:

"Elder's Curios."

Aiden swallowed, staring at the dusty window display—cluttered with oddities that seemed both familiar and foreign. The storefront felt like it remembered being owed.

Something about the shop felt different. The air around it seemed... thicker. Like the kind of stillness right before a thunderstorm.

He reached for the door handle.

And hesitated.

For the second time that day, he felt that same prickling sensation at the back of his neck. The feeling sharpened—noticed by eyes that didn't blink.

His breath hitched as he slowly turned his head, scanning the street.

At first, there was nothing.

Just empty sidewalks, a few parked cars, and the distant hum of the city beyond.

Then—

A shadow moved.

Just beyond the glow of the streetlamps, a boy stood in the alleyway, watching.

No—not a boy. The shape shifted. It was like watching a mirage—one second, it was a lanky teenager with his hands stuffed in his hoodie, and the next, a man, older, sharper, his long coat stirring slightly even though there was no wind.

Aiden's chest tightened. He knew that face.

It was the same one he had glimpsed earlier.

A flicker of movement.

Aiden blinked.

And the figure was gone.

His pulse roared in his ears.

"What the hell is going on?"

He turned back toward the shop, trying to shake off the unsettling sense of déjà vu.

Then, with a deep breath, he pushed open the door—

And stepped inside.

The Watcher in the Shadows

A small brass bell jingled as Aiden stepped inside, its cheery chime at odds with the uneasy weight in his chest.

The shop smelled of aged wood, dust, and something faintly sweet—like incense burned long ago. The dim lighting cast long shadows across the cluttered shelves, which overflowed with oddities that seemed both ancient and strangely familiar.

Aiden took a slow breath, trying to shake off the lingering chill from the alleyway.

"There was no one there."

But he didn't quite believe that.

A slight hum filled the silence—not from any machine, but from the shop itself. The air carried a weight, a pressure against his skin, as if the very walls were watching him.

As Aiden moved deeper inside, he ran his fingers along an ornate dagger, its silver hilt cold to the touch. A music box beside it began playing softly, even though he hadn't wound it. In a glass case, a book bound in something too dark to be leather seemed to shimmer in the low light.

Everything in this store felt... alive.

"Curious and bold," the ad had said.

Aiden wasn't sure if he felt bold. But he was definitely curious.

Then—

"Looking for something special, are you?"

The voice came from behind the counter, smooth and patient, as though the speaker had been expecting him.

Aiden turned sharply.

The shopkeeper stood there, watching him with dark, knowing eyes.

He was tall and wiry, with deep lines etched across his face, though his age was impossible to pin down. His hands rested lightly on the counter, fingers adorned with rings of different metals—some polished, some tarnished with time.

Aiden hesitated, suddenly unsure of what to say.

"I... I don't know yet."

The shopkeeper's lips curled in amusement. "Ah. You've got that look."

"What look?"

"Curiosity. It's a dangerous thing, you know."

Aiden frowned, shifting his weight.

"I just—"

His words died in his throat.

Because out of the corner of his eye, something moved.

A shadow flickered against the far wall—brief, barely there, but unmistakable.

Aiden's stomach clenched.

Someone was here.

"Who else is in the shop?" he asked, turning back to the shopkeeper.

The man tilted his head slightly. "Just us."

Aiden's fingers twitched. He knew what he had seen.

And more than that—he felt it.

Like before, outside. The same eerie sensation, like a presence just beyond the edge of his vision.

The shopkeeper's eyes flicked toward the doorway leading to the back of the shop.

"Then who's watching me?" Aiden asked.

The shopkeeper exhaled softly, as if debating his answer. Then, with a slight nod, he simply said:

"Someone who wants to see what you'll do next."

Entering Elder's Curios: The Door to Fate

Aiden's skin prickled.

"Someone who wants to see what I'll do next?"

The words hung in the air between him and the shopkeeper, thick with meaning Aiden couldn't yet grasp. He wanted to press for answers, demand to know who—or what—was watching him. But the way the shopkeeper held his gaze, patient yet impenetrable, made it clear that he wouldn't get a straight answer.

Instead, Aiden exhaled and forced himself to look around again.

The hum in the shop had grown stronger.

It wasn't something he could hear, exactly—it was more like a low vibration beneath his skin, a sense of tension in the air, like the moments before a lightning strike.

His feet carried him forward before he even realized it.

Deeper into the shop, past glass cases filled with rusted compasses, past a row of masks carved from dark wood, past a mirror so cracked it barely reflected his face properly.

And then—

His breath caught.

On a small pedestal, surrounded by dusty books and old trinkets, rested a golden revolver.

Its barrel gleamed faintly under the shop's dim lighting, intricate carvings winding along its surface like veins of molten gold. The handle was dark, polished, its grip wrapped in what looked like aged leather, but it was the way the entire weapon seemed to… pulse that made Aiden's fingers itch. The metal held warmth as if it remembered a trigger he hadn't pulled.

"That," the shopkeeper murmured, his voice impossibly close to Aiden's ear even though he hadn't moved, "is not just a weapon, boy. That's a choice."

Aiden swallowed, feeling his pulse match the slow, steady rhythm coming from the gun.

"What do you mean?"

The shopkeeper leaned casually against the counter, watching him. "Some objects are just objects. But others…" He paused, his fingers tapping the wooden surface. "They come with a price."

Aiden tore his eyes away from the gun long enough to glance at the books beside it.

One was thick, bound in black leather, its pages edged in golden script. Unlike the rest of the dusty tomes in the shop, this one seemed… pristine, untouched by time.

The title, embossed across the cover, sent a shiver down Aiden's spine:

The Sorcerer's Codex.

He reached for it instinctively.

As soon as his fingertips brushed the cover, the shop's dim lights flickered.

The hum in the air intensified, like something had just shifted around him. A breeze that shouldn't exist indoors swept through the store, rustling the pages of nearby books.

Aiden jerked his hand back, heart hammering.

"What was that?"

The shopkeeper merely smiled.

"It knows you, now."

Aiden's mouth felt dry.

"What the hell does that mean?"

"It means," the shopkeeper said, gesturing toward the Codex, "you've already started down this path. Whether you like it or not."

Aiden's fingers curled into fists. He didn't like this cryptic nonsense—he just wanted answers.

"What's in the book?"

The shopkeeper tilted his head, considering. Then, with a casual gesture, he flipped open the Codex. The pages fell to a diagram of twisting lines and strange symbols—unfamiliar, yet oddly familiar.

It took Aiden a moment to realize what he was looking at.

"A map?"

The shopkeeper nodded. "Of sorts. A map of something much older than this world."

Aiden ran his fingers over the golden ink, tracing the swirling lines. His head throbbed faintly, like something was pressing against his thoughts.

His gaze drifted back to the gun on the pedestal.

"Are they connected?" he asked, voice quieter now.

"Oh, very much so," the shopkeeper said. "One guides the other. One cannot function without the other."

Aiden exhaled sharply.

He should turn around, walk out of this store, and never look back.

But something inside him whispered that he wouldn't. That he couldn't.

The Codex was calling him, just as surely as the gun was.

He reached for the revolver. The room leaned a degree colder; the glass hummed with a hairline tone.

As his fingers wrapped around the grip, a sharp shock jolted up his arm.

The world tilted.

For a split second, he wasn't in the shop anymore.

He was somewhere else—somewhere vast, endless, filled with rivers of golden light stretching across the sky, like veins pulsing through the fabric of reality itself. Each current carried a cost; his footstep rang like an edit.

The hum became a roar.

His head spun, his vision darkened—

And then he was back in the shop, gasping, the gun clenched in his shaking hand.

The shopkeeper watched him with an amused expression.

"Congratulations," he said, "You've just introduced yourself to the ley lines."

The Destiny Gun and The Sorcerer's Codex

Aiden's breath came fast and uneven. His fingers were locked around the gun's grip, his palm tingling with a residual hum—as if the weapon had fused itself to him, just for that brief moment.

The world had shifted. He knew it. He had felt it.

"What the hell just happened?" he gasped, looking up at the shopkeeper.

The man gave him a knowing smile, folding his arms. "The ley lines don't react to just anyone, kid."

"Ley lines?" Aiden repeated, his voice barely above a whisper.

The shopkeeper gestured toward the open Codex, where the golden lines on the page pulsed faintly, like veins filled with liquid fire.

"Every world has them—rivers of energy, flowing beneath the surface of reality. Some people go their whole lives never noticing them. Others..." He paused, tapping a ringed finger against his chin. "Others feel them, whether they want to or not." They conduct the change; something else decides it.

Aiden's mouth felt dry.

"And you're saying I can... feel them?"

"You tell me," the shopkeeper said simply.

Aiden looked down at the gun in his hands.

It was warm. Too warm—not like metal should feel. The intricate carvings along the barrel seemed to shift in the dim light, as if the gun was breathing in tandem with him.

"This isn't normal," Aiden muttered.

The shopkeeper chuckled. "You're catching on."

Aiden glanced at the Codex again. The map of golden lines was detailed, spanning across an unfamiliar world, with certain points glowing brighter than others. His mind reeled as he tried to process it.

"Is this a map of ley lines?" he asked, pointing at it.

"Not just ley lines," the shopkeeper corrected. "Nexus points. Convergences of power, places where the weave of fate is easier to... alter."

Aiden's fingers twitched.

"And this gun is connected to that?"

"Oh, deeply," the shopkeeper said, watching Aiden closely. "Some say it draws its power from the lines themselves. Others think it was made from the stuff of ley lines—gold pulled straight from the currents of fate."

Aiden exhaled sharply, shaking his head.

"You're telling me this thing can change fate?"

The shopkeeper's expression turned thoughtful. "It can alter threads, yes. Some doors it can open. Others it can close. But change fate?" He smiled slightly. "That depends on who's holding it."

Aiden swallowed hard, gripping the gun tighter.

For the first time since walking into the shop, he felt the weight of his decision.

"Why me?" he asked.

"It's not about why," the shopkeeper said. "It's about what comes next."

Aiden stared down at the Codex, his eyes tracing the strange symbols lining the map's edges. The writing wasn't in English—or in any language he had ever seen before—but something about it felt... familiar.

He ran a hand over the leather cover, feeling the fine grain beneath his fingertips.

"You said these go together," he said. "The gun and the Codex."

The shopkeeper nodded. "The gun is the tool. The Codex is the guide." One writes in the world; one records the cost.

Aiden frowned. "Guide to what?"

The shopkeeper's gaze darkened slightly. "To whatever comes next."

Aiden wanted to press him for more, but before he could—

The brass bell above the shop's door chimed.

A cold breeze swept through the store.

Aiden turned sharply.

A tall figure had stepped inside, the dim light casting his face into shadow. A wide-brimmed hat sat low over his forehead, obscuring his features, but his eyes—sharp, unblinking—locked onto Aiden immediately.

The energy in the store shifted.

Aiden knew who it was before the shopkeeper even said his name.

"Ah," the shopkeeper murmured, his voice unreadable. "Pecos."

Pecos Observes: The Timewalker's Perspective

The moment Pecos stepped inside, the air grew heavier.

Aiden didn't know why, but the energy in the shop changed—as if reality itself had momentarily paused to acknowledge his arrival.

The man's silhouette was tall and lean, his wide-brimmed hat casting a long shadow across the wooden floorboards. He wore a coat that looked both ancient and brand-new at the same time, its fabric shifting under the dim light in a way Aiden couldn't quite place.

But it was his eyes that struck Aiden the most.

Sharp. Unblinking. Old.

Not old in the way his grandfather had been old—this was something else entirely. It was like Pecos had seen centuries, yet still remained untouched by them.

The shopkeeper didn't react, merely folding his hands on the counter, watching the newcomer with mild curiosity.

"Didn't expect you so soon," the shopkeeper said, his voice even.

Pecos didn't answer immediately. He let his gaze drift over Aiden, then the gun in his hand, then the open Codex on the counter. His lips pressed into a faint smirk.

"So," Pecos finally spoke, his voice smooth yet strangely layered, as if he was speaking from more than one point in time. "It chose him."

Aiden felt his grip tighten on the gun.

"Chose?" he echoed, his voice laced with tension.

Pecos took a slow step forward, the worn leather of his boots barely making a sound on the old wooden floor.

"This isn't the first time I've seen someone pick that up," he murmured, his eyes flickering to the Destiny Gun. "But I'll tell you this, kid—every time it finds a new hand to rest in, things tend to… shift."

Aiden swallowed hard.

He wasn't sure if Pecos was threatening him or warning him.

"Who are you?" Aiden asked, forcing himself to stand his ground.

Pecos tilted his head slightly, as if amused by the question.

"Just someone who's walked this path before," he said. "And someone who knows what happens next."

The shopkeeper sighed. "Come to give a speech, have you?"

Pecos chuckled. "Wouldn't be the first time. Won't be the last."

Aiden frowned.

"Enough with the riddles," he snapped, the weight of everything pressing on him at once. "If you know something, just tell me. What is this gun? What is this book? And why the hell does it feel like I've just stepped into a place I can't walk back from?"

Pecos watched him carefully, the amusement in his gaze fading just a little.

For the first time, he looked… almost curious.

"Because you have," he said simply. "Once you touch the gun, the ley lines touch you back." They remember who pressed first.

Aiden's stomach dropped.

"What does that mean?"

Pecos didn't answer right away. Instead, he reached into his coat pocket and pulled out something small—a coin.

The sight of it made Aiden's breath hitch.

It was identical to the Lost King's Coin his grandfather had once shown him—the same swirling pattern around an unblinking eye, the same worn edges, as if time had eroded it, yet left its markings untouched.

Pecos rolled the coin between his fingers effortlessly before flipping it into the air. Its spin left a thin ring in the air, like a groove cut into a moment.

The second it spun—something shifted in the room.

The shop seemed to dim and brighten all at once, the golden filigree in the Codex glowing brighter for just a moment. Aiden felt it, that strange pull in his chest, as if something deep inside him had just been… measured.

The coin landed in Pecos's palm without a sound.

"You ever hear of echoes, kid?" Pecos asked, slipping the coin back into his coat.

Aiden hesitated. "Like… sound?"

Pecos shook his head.

"No. Echoes in time. Things that shouldn't still exist, but do. Paths that should've closed, but didn't. The gun, the Codex, the ley lines—they don't just move forward. They ripple. And when you take a step into something bigger than you, those ripples? They find you."

Aiden's chest felt tight.

"You're saying… I can't just walk away from this."

Pecos gave a half-smile. "You could try. But the ley lines don't forget. And neither does the gun."

Aiden looked down at the Destiny Gun, the golden etchings along its barrel pulsing faintly, as if alive.

He had felt something when he touched it. Something shift.

And now, hearing Pecos say it outright...

He knew.

There was no going back.

"So what now?" Aiden asked, his voice quieter.

Pecos studied him for a long moment before shrugging.

"That depends on you," he said. "The ley lines chose you for a reason. Now it's up to you to figure out what that reason is."

Aiden's head swam with questions he didn't have answers to.

But one thing was clear.

This wasn't just about gold anymore.

It wasn't even about treasure.

It was about something bigger—something older than the world he knew.

And whether he was ready or not...

He was part of it now.

The Transaction: Fate Sealed

Aiden's fingers curled around the Destiny Gun, his mind racing.

Pecos's words echoed in his head.

"The ley lines chose you for a reason."

He didn't feel chosen—he felt like he had stumbled into something far bigger than himself, something he didn't understand and wasn't sure he wanted to.

The shopkeeper leaned against the counter, watching the scene unfold with quiet amusement. "Well, this is turning out to be a lively morning."

Aiden swallowed, shifting his grip on the gun. "I don't... I don't know what to do with this."

"You'll figure it out," Pecos said, flicking a speck of dust off his coat. "Or you won't. Either way, the wheels are turning now."

Aiden turned to the shopkeeper, hoping for something—anything—that would ground him.

"What's the price?" he asked.

The shopkeeper smiled faintly. "For the gun?"

Aiden nodded.

"It's not for sale," the man said simply.

Aiden blinked. "But—"

"It's already yours," the shopkeeper interrupted. "You think things like this operate on cash? Please. That gun's been waiting for you, boy. The real question is, what are you willing to give for it?"

The words sent a chill through Aiden's spine.

He looked at the Codex, still glowing faintly on the counter.

"And the book?"

The shopkeeper glanced at Pecos, who merely raised an eyebrow, before turning his attention back to Aiden. "You'll need it."

Aiden -expression. "That's not an answer."

The shopkeeper tilted his head, considering.

Then he slid the Codex forward, tapping one finger against its cover. "I'll make you a deal, kid. The Codex goes with the gun—it always has. And right now, you're standing on the threshold of something much larger than yourself. So, here's the trade…"

Aiden leaned in slightly.

"You take the gun. You take the Codex. And you take responsibility for what comes next."

Aiden's throat felt tight.

"That's it?" he asked, unsure whether to believe it.

The shopkeeper's expression darkened slightly. "That's everything." Payment wasn't coins—it was consent to carry the outcomes.

Aiden hesitated.

He should walk away.

He knew it.

But deep down, something in him whispered that he wasn't supposed to.

That this moment had been waiting for him—just as much as he had been waiting for it.

Slowly, he reached for the Codex.

As soon as his fingers brushed the cover, a pulse of warmth spread through his hand, like the first ember of a fire catching onto dry wood.

The deal was made.

The shop lights flickered, the golden etchings on the gun pulsed one last time, and the hum in the air settled into a quiet, almost expectant stillness.

The transaction was sealed.

Pecos let out a low chuckle.

"Well. Guess there's no going back now."

Aiden exhaled slowly, feeling the weight of the moment settle onto his shoulders. He slipped the gun into his bag, tucking the Codex safely beside it.

The shopkeeper gave him one last look.

"You've got questions," he said. "And you'll find answers. But remember, kid—answers always come with a cost."

Aiden nodded.

Then, without another word, he turned toward the door—toward whatever waited for him outside.

As he reached for the handle, he hesitated one last time, glancing back.

Pecos was watching him closely, flipping his coin through his fingers.

"One last thing, kid," he said, his tone unreadable. "Don't go thinking you're the only one out there looking for that gun." Some hunt the gun; some hunt its edits.

Aiden's stomach dropped.

But before he could ask what that meant, Pecos tossed the coin toward him.

Instinctively, Aiden caught it.

The moment his fingers closed around the metal, a familiar hum pulsed through him—not just from the coin, but from something bigger.

He looked down.

The coin was identical to the one his grandfather had once given him.

The Lost King's Coin.

He looked back up—

But Pecos was already gone.

Aiden stepped out of Elder's Curios, the heavy wooden door swinging shut behind him with a low creak. The second his foot touched the sidewalk, the air outside felt different.

The city's usual morning sounds—cars idling at intersections, the chatter of pedestrians, the distant wail of a siren—all felt like they were happening through a thin veil, slightly distorted, slightly wrong.

He pulled the strap of his bag tighter across his chest, his mind still reeling from what had just happened.

The gun. The Codex. The ley lines.

None of it made sense, yet all of it felt real. Too real.

And then there was Pecos.

Aiden's fingers tightened around the coin still in his palm. It felt warm —like it had been in someone's hand for hours, absorbing body heat—but that wasn't possible. He shoved it into his pocket and started walking, keeping his pace brisk.

The streets of Crescent Avenue weren't usually crowded this early in the day, but as Aiden moved, he became aware of something else.

Something… off.

The further he walked, the more he felt it—that prickling sensation at the back of his neck.

The feeling of being watched.

He kept his eyes forward, resisting the urge to look over his shoulder. It was probably nothing. He was just on edge after everything that had happened in the shop. His mind was running wild, making him paranoid.

Right?

He turned a corner.

A flash of movement in his peripheral vision.

His pulse spiked.

Aiden whipped his head around—

Nothing.

The sidewalk behind him was empty. Just a few parked cars, the glow of a convenience store sign, a pigeon pecking at the ground.

He exhaled slowly, forcing himself to relax. Calm down.

But his gut told him something else.

His gut told him that he wasn't alone.

He picked up his pace, cutting across the street without waiting for the light to change. A car horn blared, but he ignored it, his focus narrowing to the rhythm of his footsteps, the shifting weight of the Destiny Gun in his bag, the steady hammering of his heart.

Then—

A shadow moved again.

This time, across the reflection of a glass storefront.

Aiden's breath caught in his throat.

He stopped walking.

Turned.

The alleyway across the street was empty.

But the air felt charged, like someone had just been standing there. Watching. Waiting.

Aiden gritted his teeth. Okay, screw this.

He pulled his hood up and started walking faster.

He needed to get home. Now.

First Night with the Gun: The Dream of Ley Lines

Aiden didn't remember falling asleep.

One moment, he was sitting on his bed, flipping through the Codex, trying to decipher the golden maps and strange symbols. The next, the world blurred—

And he was somewhere else.

A vast, endless expanse stretched before him. The sky wasn't a sky—it was a web.

Threads of golden light crisscrossed above and below, weaving into infinite patterns, stretching into horizons that didn't exist.

The ley lines.

He was standing on one.

The golden path beneath his feet pulsed, and as he took a step forward, the entire web of lines shifted, like ripples in a pond.

Aiden.

The voice wasn't spoken. It slipped into his mind like a thought he didn't have.

He turned.

A figure stood at the center of the shifting lines.

Their face was hidden in shadow, their form flickering—sometimes tall, sometimes short, sometimes impossibly thin, as if they weren't bound to a single shape.

"Who are you?" Aiden's voice came out steady, but his pulse raced.

The figure tilted its head.

"The bearer of the Destiny Gun is bound to the ley lines."

Aiden felt the gun at his hip—though he hadn't been carrying it before.

"Beware, Aiden."

The golden threads around him shifted violently, twisting, tangling, breaking apart.

"Every shot fired alters the weave." Edits don't erase the bill; they forward it.

The threads snapped.

Aiden fell.

The sky of golden rivers rushed toward him—

He hit the ground gasping, his body drenched in sweat.

His window breathed once; the room forgot then remembered his name.

The Codex was open on his desk, its pages glowing faintly.

The words on the page hadn't been there before.

"Every choice has a cost. The Destiny Gun remembers." So does the ledger that logs it.

Aiden stared at the book, his heart hammering.

He wasn't just imagining things.

Something had changed.

And whether he was ready or not…

He had already taken his first step into the unknown.

CHAPTER 2: THE GUN'S FIRST ALTERATION

Aiden sat at his desk, staring at the three objects before him—the Destiny Gun, The Sorcerer's Codex, and Pecos's coin. The golden glow from his desk lamp made them seem almost too vivid, their details sharper than he remembered. He didn't need another artifact; he needed proof of what changed when he touched it.

Outside, the night was still. Too still. Normally, the city hummed with distant life—passing cars, the occasional bark of a dog, the far-off wail of sirens. But tonight, it felt like the world was holding its breath. It felt noticed, like silence holding its breath for his decision.

The gun lay silent, its surface catching the light in a way that made it look almost alive. The Codex sat open beside it, revealing a web of twisting golden lines—lines that conduct the change; something else decides it—etched onto thick parchment. It keeps verdicts; it doesn't give orders. Pecos's coin sat between them, a dull gleam against the wood.

Aiden exhaled slowly. He hadn't touched the gun since he got home.

"It's just a gun."

But he knew that wasn't true. Not anymore.

He leaned forward, running a thumb over Pecos's coin. It was warm, as if it had been sitting in someone's palm moments before, but that wasn't possible. The symbol—a swirling pattern encircling an unblinking eye—felt familiar in a way that made his stomach twist.

"The gun doesn't pick just anyone."

Pecos's words lingered in his mind.

But why him?

A soft clicking sound broke the silence.

Aiden turned, finding Blu standing in the doorway, his large brown eyes reflecting the dim light. His tail flicked once, then he padded into the room, sniffing the air.

Aiden gave a tired smile. "You always know when I'm overthinking things, huh?"

Blu didn't wag his tail like usual. Instead, his nose twitched toward the gun, and his body tensed.

Aiden blinked. Blu wasn't looking at him. He was looking at the gun.

"Blu?" Aiden whispered, suddenly uneasy.

The dog took a step back, his ears flattening. His gaze darted between Aiden and the Codex, then back to the gun. His body language screamed one thing:

Something isn't right.

Aiden's pulse quickened. "Buddy?"

Blu let out a low whine. His droopy ears twitched, and his tail tucked slightly between his legs. Then he did something he had never done before.

He bowed his head.

Aiden's stomach dropped. Blu was a laid-back dog, always relaxed, always eager for treats or belly rubs. He didn't act like this—not even during thunderstorms.

But now, he was lowering his head, eyes locked on the gun like it was something bigger than him.

Aiden swallowed. "Hey, it's just... a dumb piece of metal, okay?"

Blu didn't move.

The silence stretched.

As if recognizing rank—object first, then owner.

Then, without warning, the Codex shifted on its own.

Aiden flinched. The pages fluttered, as if caught in an invisible breeze. Then they settled, revealing a passage written in looping golden script.

Aiden leaned closer, his breath catching as he read:

"The first shot is never the last. The weave is never untouched."

The book was logging, not warning.

The words glowed softly, and as Aiden reached out, his fingers brushed the ink.

A faint vibration ran through his hand, like touching the surface of a ringing bell. The room dropped two degrees; the lamp filament sang.

His heartbeat quickened.

Blu took another step back, letting out a deep, uneasy growl.

The air felt thicker now, charged with something unseen.

Aiden tore his gaze away from the book, his eyes landing back on the Destiny Gun.

It looked normal. But he could feel it now—a hum just beneath his skin, a pull that hadn't been there before.

He licked his lips.

It was waiting.

He reached out, wrapping his fingers around the grip.

Heat flashed through his palm, racing up his arm.

The air around him shimmered, warping just slightly.

Aiden's breath hitched.

He hesitated—what if this changed something? What if this wasn't meant to be touched?

But the longer he held it, the more it felt like it belonged there.

He took a slow, steadying breath—

And pulled the trigger. No bullet. The edit went outward instead.

Reality Shift – Touching the Ley Lines

The moment Aiden pulled the trigger, the world didn't explode.

There was no gunfire, no violent recoil, no bullet tearing through his desk. Instead—

A golden ripple expanded outward, silent but impossibly heavy, like a shockwave that didn't disturb the air but bent reality itself.

The ripple passed through him, through Blu, through the walls, the floor, the ceiling—like they weren't even there.

Aiden's breath hitched.

For a moment, everything was still.

Then—

His room shifted.

It wasn't immediate—it was subtle, like stepping into a house you've lived in your whole life only to realize the furniture is just slightly wrong.

Aiden's desk had moved—not by much, just a few inches to the left. But he hadn't touched it.

His window blinds were open. A streetlamp outside now faced the wrong corner.

They had been closed a second ago.

The air turned sharp—static before a storm.

Aiden's fingers clenched around the gun's grip. "What... just happened?"

Blu whimpered, his body still low to the ground. His paws shifted uneasily, like he was standing on unsteady terrain.

Aiden turned his head—and froze.

A faint glowing line ran across the floorboards, pulsing softly with golden light.

His stomach twisted. That wasn't there before.

The glow intensified, like a heartbeat matching his own pulse.

Blu let out a sharp bark, his tail tucking fully between his legs. His gaze was locked on the glowing seam—like he saw something Aiden couldn't.

Aiden swallowed hard. He had to touch it.

His body moved before his mind could stop him.

Fingers stretched forward.

A whisper in his thoughts: Seams show where an edit can still be touched.

He barely brushed the golden light when—

The world shattered.

The Vision of the Ley Lines

Aiden was falling.

Not through space. Not through time.

Through something else.

A vast, endless expanse stretched before him—a web of golden threads, crisscrossing through the air like a spider's web spun across infinity.

The lines pulsed with power, each thread interwoven, twisting, shifting —alive.

Some were bright and strong, others were frayed, unstable, snapping and flickering out like dying embers.

And in the distance—

Something watched him.

Aiden felt it before he saw it—a presence, massive and unblinking, just beyond the edges of his vision.

Slowly, he turned his head.

And there it was.

A pair of enormous, golden eyes, staring at him from within the ley lines. Not author, not animal—an auditor.

A voice slipped into his mind, deep and distant, as if spoken from outside time itself.

"You are seen." Seen means indexed.

Aiden's chest tightened. His lungs seized.

His vision swam.

And then—

He slammed back into his body.

Reality Snaps Back – But Something Has Changed

Aiden's back hit the floor hard.

His vision blurred, his ears rang, his breath came in ragged gasps.

He was back in his room.

Back in his reality.

But something wasn't right.

Blu stood a few feet away, staring at him with glowing gold eyes.

Aiden blinked. His head pounded, his chest heaved—but he wasn't imagining it.

Blu's eyes were wrong.

Not entirely, not yet—but the flecks of gold in them were brighter now, swirling faintly like ink in water. Edits pick companions before they pick consequences.

Aiden's pulse spiked.

"Blu?" he rasped.

Blu whined, his body flickering—for a split second, Aiden swore his fur looked translucent, shifting between solid and something else.

Then, just as quickly, he was normal again.

But he wasn't.

Aiden dragged himself up, heart slamming against his ribs.

The Codex lay on his desk, its pages flipping wildly as if caught in a storm.

The glowing seam on the floor was gone.

But the air still hummed, vibrating like a plucked string.

And in the depths of his mind, the voice whispered once more:

"You are seen."

Aiden's breath was still ragged when the air in his room shifted again.

It wasn't like before—no golden ripples, no visions of ley lines.

This was different.

The temperature dropped, and a faint scent of gunpowder and dust filled the air.

Then—

"Well, kid. That didn't take long."

Aiden whipped around, heart hammering.

Pecos stood in the doorway.

His coat was the same—a worn duster, stained with time—but his expression was different. Less smug, more… wary.

Aiden- "You knew this would happen."

Pecos sighed, stepping further into the room. His boots made no sound against the wooden floor.

"You didn't just pull the trigger," he said. "You sent out a signal." Signals travel faster than warnings.

Aiden stiffened. "What do you mean?"

Pecos moved closer, his eyes flicking toward the spot where the glowing seam had been. He ran a hand through his scruffy beard.

"The ley lines aren't just roads, kid. They're echoes of fate. And every time you fire that thing…" He exhaled sharply. "Someone listens."

Aiden's stomach turned. "Who?"

Pecos didn't answer immediately. Instead, he crouched beside Blu, who hadn't moved since the shift.

The basset hound's golden-tinged eyes tracked Pecos warily, ears twitching at some silent sound Aiden couldn't hear.

Pecos studied him. His face was unreadable, but Aiden didn't miss the way his jaw tensed.

"Well, that's interesting."

Aiden narrowed his eyes. "What's happening to him?"

Pecos didn't answer right away. He just stood, stretching his shoulders, like this whole thing was a damn inconvenience.

"Power leaves echoes, kid. Some louder than others."

Aiden's expression. ~ "You keep saying that, but it doesn't mean anything."

Pecos gave him a long look. Then he tossed something at Aiden.

Aiden caught it on instinct.

Another coin.

Not like the first.

This one was darker, heavier. Its etched markings weren't swirling this time—they were jagged, fractured. Fractures remember breaks the way grooves remember songs.

"You're not the only one out there with a gun like that," Pecos said. "And now? They know about you."

The Gun's True Cost – And Aiden's Choice

Aiden stared at the coin, his stomach tightening.

"They?" His voice was quieter now.

Pecos tilted his head, expression unreadable.

"Ley line wielders. Hunters. People who know better than to play with fate the way you just did." He nodded toward the Destiny Gun. "That thing? It's not just a weapon. It's an invitation." Admission is responsibility.

Aiden swallowed hard. "An invitation to what?"

Pecos smirked, but there was no amusement in it.

"To the kind of trouble you don't get to walk away from."

Silence stretched between them.

Aiden looked down at Blu again.

The dog was still watching him, still not normal.

Maybe he never would be again.

His fingers tightened around the coin. He had done this.

His actions had changed something.

And now, he wasn't the only one who knew.

The gun in his hand felt heavier than before.

Aiden exhaled slowly. Then, without another word, he turned toward his desk.

His phone sat there, screen glowing in the dim light.

Kyle. Sarah. Mark.

People he trusted. People who might not believe him—but who would come anyway.

He picked up the phone. Calling witnesses records the choice twice.

Pressed the call button.

"Yo, Aiden!" Kyle's voice came through immediately. "What's up?"

Aiden took a breath.

"Meet me at the park," he said. "There's something I need to show you."

Kyle laughed. "What, you finally learn how to dunk?"

Aiden exhaled.

"Just get there," he said. He hung up.

And with that, he had made his choice.

The hunt had begun.

CHAPTER 3: GATHERING THE CREW

Aiden woke with a start. Today wasn't about collecting; it was about telling—and choosing who could stand next to the truth.

His heart pounded in his chest, his skin damp with sweat. The world felt off—like he had woken up in a version of his room that wasn't quite his own. Like a room that knows it's being watched.

He sat up, rubbing his temples. The remnants of a dream—or a vision—lingered in his mind. Golden threads twisting into knots, fraying, snapping. A voice—deep, distant, and ancient—had whispered his name.

"You are seen."

Aiden exhaled, glancing toward his desk.

The Destiny Gun lay there, motionless, but he could still feel its weight in his mind. The Sorcerer's Codex rested beside it, pages still open to the passage that had burned itself into his memory:

"The first shot is never the last. The weave is never untouched."

The Codex keeps verdicts; it doesn't give orders.

And Blu—Blu was watching him.

The basset hound sat near the window, his golden-tinged eyes unblinking in the dim morning light. He didn't move like a normal dog anymore. He was too still, too aware. As if the object outranked its owner.

Aiden swallowed hard. The gun had done something to him.

"Blu?" he asked, voice rough.

Blu tilted his head, but his body flickered—just for an instant—between solid and something translucent, something shifting. Stabilize, or slip—those were the only two directions.

Aiden's stomach dropped. It wasn't just the gun. The ley lines had changed Blu, too.

The Weight of the Decision

Aiden swung his legs over the side of his bed, running a hand through his hair. The past twenty-four hours had rewritten his entire reality.

The gun. The Codex. The glowing seam in his floor that had vanished, but left an imprint in his mind.

And now Pecos's warning.

"You're not the only one out there with a gun like that. And now? They know about you."

Aiden glanced at his phone. The screen was cracked at the corner—a result of dropping it the night before, hands shaking after everything that had happened.

He had wanted to call his friends then. But what could he even say?

"Hey, guys. I picked up an old gun from a creepy shop, and now reality is unraveling around me."

Yeah. No way.

But he also knew he couldn't do this alone.

Blu stood up suddenly, his nails clicking against the wooden floor. His ears perked, his head turning toward the door.

Then Aiden heard it, too.

Footsteps.

Not coming from inside the house.

From the alley outside his window.

His breath caught in his throat. He moved fast—grabbing the gun from the desk and moving toward the window. Slowly, he peered outside.

The alley was empty.

But the air felt heavy, charged.

He couldn't explain how he knew. But someone had been there. Watching.

Return pings come as silence that leans in.

Blu let out a low, almost human-like growl.

Aiden clenched his jaw.

This was happening. Whether he wanted it to or not.

He turned back toward his phone, opened his texts, and typed:

MEET AT THE PARK. NEED TO TALK. ASAP.

He hit send to Kyle, Sarah, and Mark before he could second-guess himself. Calling witnesses records the choice twice.

Aiden stared at the message, his stomach twisting.

They deserved to know. But once he told them… there was no taking it back.

Outside, the wind shifted.

Somewhere in the distance, a golden thread snapped.

Aiden sat on his bike, gripping the handlebars tightly as he rode toward Old Creek Park. The morning air was crisp, but thick with an energy he couldn't shake. Where seams could still be touched and edits still moved.

The message had been sent. There was no turning back now.

Blu trotted beside him, unnaturally silent for a dog of his size. He kept pace with Aiden easily, his movements more fluid than they should have been.

Every so often, Aiden would glance down at him, and for a fraction of a second, Blu's body seemed to flicker—almost translucent.

Aiden clenched his jaw. What had he done to his best friend?

The gun was tucked into the inner pocket of his jacket, but even without touching it, he could feel it. It wasn't just an object anymore. It was something alive.

Something waiting.

The Meeting Spot

The park was mostly empty—too early for the usual joggers and dog walkers. Good. Proof reads cleaner without a crowd.

Aiden rolled to a stop near the old concrete picnic tables, the ones where he, Kyle, Sarah, and Mark had spent countless summers scheming up adventures that never really led anywhere.

But today? Today was different.

Kyle was the first to arrive.

Tall, with messy dark hair and an easy confidence, Kyle was always the first one to jump headfirst into something without thinking.

He spotted Aiden and jogged over, grinning.

"Yo, dude, what's with the all-caps text? You finally found a way to make money without working?"

Aiden let out a breath. "Not exactly."

Kyle's gaze flickered to Blu, then back to Aiden. "Okay, serious face. What's up?"

Before Aiden could answer, Sarah and Mark arrived together.

Sarah, sharp-eyed and skeptical as always, crossed her arms the second she saw Aiden's expression. "This better not be some elaborate joke, Aiden. I was in the middle of studying."

Mark, quiet but always noticing everything, pushed up his glasses. "And you sounded serious. That's new."

Aiden hesitated.

How did he even begin to explain this?

Blu sat beside him, his glowing gold eyes watching them all.

Kyle noticed first. "Okay, uh—what's up with Blu's eyes?"

Sarah frowned. "Yeah, that… doesn't look normal."

Aiden exhaled sharply. "Yeah. Nothing's been normal since yesterday."

He reached into his jacket.

The moment he pulled out the Destiny Gun, the air seemed to shift.

The light caught the golden engravings along the barrel, the intricate carvings shimmering faintly.

Sarah took an instinctive step back. "Aiden, what the hell is that?"

Mark's brow furrowed. "A gun?"

Kyle, instead of being alarmed, leaned in with genuine curiosity. "That thing looks old as hell. Where'd you get it?"

Aiden tightened his grip. "That's… complicated."

Blu let out a low whine.

Aiden took a breath. "Look, I need you guys to listen. And I need you to believe me."

A pause.

Then Kyle smirked. "Dude, when have we ever not believed you?"

Sarah muttered, "I can list at least five times—"

Kyle waved her off. "Go on, Aiden. What's the deal?"

Aiden hesitated. Then, finally, he said:

"This gun doesn't just shoot bullets." It doesn't fire bullets; it pushes an edit.

He turned and aimed at a small rock near the tree line.

Kyle laughed. "What, you gonna—"

Aiden pulled the trigger.

The air rippled.

The rock didn't shatter.

It shifted.

In the span of a heartbeat, the dull gray stone was replaced with pure, glimmering gold.

The ripple spread outward, like something unseen had taken notice.

Aiden lowered the gun. "Now do you believe me?"

Silence.

The rock—now gold—sat glinting in the morning light. Somewhere behind them, a bench plaque now bore a different name.

Kyle took a step forward, mouth slightly open. He crouched and reached out, tapping the rock with his knuckle. The metallic clink rang sharp in the quiet air.

"Holy—"

He grabbed it, turning it over in his hands, eyes wide. "Dude. This is… this is real gold?"

Aiden nodded stiffly. His grip on the Destiny Gun tightened.

Mark took a slow breath, rubbing the back of his head. "Okay. I'm assuming that wasn't some cheap magician's trick?"

Sarah crossed her arms, expression unreadable. "That wasn't just chemistry or physics, was it?"

Aiden shook his head. "No. This thing doesn't just shoot bullets. It changes things."

Kyle let out a laugh—not one of amusement, but of pure disbelief. "Bro. This is insane."

Mark frowned, turning to Aiden. "What happens if you shoot something alive?"

The question sent a shiver down Aiden's spine. He hadn't thought of that yet.

Blu let out a low growl, his ears twitching. The wind picked up, rustling through the trees. The air felt heavier.

Aiden took a breath. "That's not even the worst part."

Sarah raised a brow. "Oh, great. There's more?"

Aiden nodded. "Every time I pull the trigger, something happens."

Mark's eyes narrowed. "What kind of 'something'?"

Before Aiden could answer, the Codex flipped open on its own.

The pages fluttered wildly before settling. New words had appeared in golden ink.

Kyle read it aloud:

"Every shot echoes. And echoes bring seekers."

The book was logging, not warning.

Aiden's stomach dropped.

Blu let out a sharp bark, his body tensing.

Aiden felt it now too—that same sensation from last night.

Like something was watching them.

The Disturbance

Aiden turned toward the tree line, eyes scanning the shadows.

Nothing.

But the air was wrong.

The golden rock hummed faintly, like the transformation was still rippling through reality.

Then—

The light shifted.

For a fraction of a second, the trees seemed to bend inward, their edges warping like heat waves. Not an author—an auditor.

Blu barked again, his fur bristling.

Kyle stepped back. "Uh. Guys? What the hell was that?"

Mark adjusted his glasses, staring at the trees. "I think… I think we just triggered something."

Sarah took an uneasy step closer to Aiden. "Tell me this doesn't happen every time."

Aiden's fingers itched toward the gun's grip. "Only when I fire it."

The air thickened. The world felt too quiet—like something was listening.

Then, Blu did something Aiden had never seen before.

He spoke.

"They're here." Indexed becomes present, and present arrives armed.

*****

Aiden's breath caught in his throat.

Blu had spoken. Not a growl, not a whimper—actual words.

Kyle staggered backward. "What the—Blu just talked!"

Mark's face paled. "Did… did anyone else hear that?"

Blu's golden eyes gleamed faintly in the dim light. He turned toward the trees.

Aiden followed his gaze—and that's when he saw it.

A man in a long coat, flipping a coin.

Pecos.

Aiden exhaled sharply. "You again?"

Pecos strolled toward them, boots making no sound on the dirt path. He twirled the coin between his fingers before catching it.

"You're moving fast, kid. Maybe too fast."

Sarah, Kyle, and Mark all stared at him.

Kyle blinked. "Uh. Who's the cowboy?"

Pecos tipped his hat slightly. "Just someone who knows when fate's being tampered with."

Sarah scoffed. "Great. Another cryptic guy."

Aiden turned to Pecos. "You said if I used the gun, people would notice. I'm guessing that's happening now?"

Pecos smirked. "Took you long enough to figure that out."

Blu let out a sharp whine, his ears twitching.

Aiden turned back toward the trees—and froze.

A shadow moved in the distance.

Not a person.

Something else.

Pecos sighed. "And here I was hoping you had more time."

Aiden's throat tightened. "Who are they?"

"Some chase the gun; others chase the edits it leaves behind."

Pecos caught his coin and held it up to the light. The metal gleamed, dark and ancient.

"You're about to meet the ones who listen when fate is rewritten."

The air grew dense, thick like a storm about to break.

Aiden's skin prickled. He didn't need Pecos to spell it out—something was coming.

Blu stood rigid, his golden eyes locked on the shifting shadows beyond the trees. His fur bristled, and the way his body flickered slightly at the edges made Aiden's stomach turn.

Sarah, Kyle, and Mark were staring now, too.

Sarah's voice was tight. "Aiden… what exactly did you do?"

Kyle, ever the reckless one, took a step forward, squinting at the tree line. "Look, if someone's trying to mug us or whatever—"

Aiden grabbed his arm, yanking him back. "Kyle. Don't."

Something shifted in the trees.

A shape—tall, cloaked in layers of shadow that weren't quite attached to its body.

A second figure appeared. Then a third.

No faces. Only silhouettes, wrapped in the flickering distortion of the ley lines.

Pecos clicked his tongue. "Well. That's a problem."

The figures didn't move toward them—not yet. They just… stood there, as if waiting. Watching.

Blu growled—low, guttural, almost human.

And then—

The tallest of the figures spoke.

"The ley lines will correct what has been altered." Correction takes payment.

The voice wasn't human. It was layered, like multiple people speaking at once, rippling across time itself.

The Weavers were gone.

But something remained in the air.

Aiden's breathing was shallow, his fingers still wrapped tightly around the Destiny Gun. His heart hammered against his ribs—not from fear, but from something heavier.

A presence.

The ground beneath his feet felt wrong, off-balance, as if the ley lines were still stretched too thin, trembling from his interference.

Kyle let out a breathy, nervous laugh, running a hand through his hair. "Screw. That. I don't know what they were, but I vote we never see them again."

Sarah, arms crossed, wasn't laughing. "We just watched reality bend. We should be figuring out what's happening, not running from it."

Mark adjusted his glasses. "They didn't just appear because of the gun. They responded to something else." His eyes flickered toward Aiden. "To you."

Aiden barely heard them. His focus drifted to the ground beneath his feet.

A thin golden crack pulsed softly in the dirt where the Weavers had stood. It was no larger than a footprint, but it wasn't natural. It glowed faintly, twisting like a vein of molten metal in the earth.

Then—it pulsed.

Aiden flinched. He stepped back, but no one else seemed to notice it. Not Kyle, not Sarah, not even Mark.

Only Blu did.

The dog whined low in his throat, his ears flat against his head. He wasn't looking at the crack—he was looking at Aiden.

Aiden's grip tightened around the gun, his fingers tingling with something he didn't understand.

And then, from the edge of the clearing—

A slow clinking sound.

Pecos.

The old gunslinger leaned against the wooden post of a streetlamp, flipping his coin, his expression unreadable. "Well," he mused, "that's one way to introduce yourself to the ley lines."

Aiden stiffened. "You were watching?"

Pecos shrugged. "More like listening. And kid—" he nodded at the golden crack still shimmering in the dirt—"so was everything else."

The air dropped two degrees; a nearby compass app spun once and settled.

Kyle groaned. "Okay, who the hell is this guy?"

Sarah shot Pecos a hard look. "Are you going to explain what's happening? Or are you just here to be cryptic again?"

Pecos chuckled, flicking the coin toward Aiden. Instinctively, Aiden caught it. The metal was warm.

Pecos's smirk faded slightly. "Ley lines don't like being tugged at, kid. Pull one thread, you unravel things you never meant to." He tapped his temple, watching Aiden closely. "And some things start lookin' back."

Aiden swallowed hard.

The crack in the ground pulsed one last time—then faded.

But Aiden could still feel it.

Waiting.

Watching.

Pecos sighed, stretching like a man already tired of the conversation. "Best get on home, kid. You got bigger problems than Weavers now."

"Signals arrive before sense."

And just like that, he turned and walked away.

Kyle muttered under his breath, "I hate that guy."

Mark's gaze lingered on Aiden. "You felt something, didn't you?"

Aiden hesitated, his fingers curling around the Destiny Gun.

Yeah. He felt something.

And it wasn't gone.

It was just beginning.

Kyle cursed under his breath. "Nope. Nooope."

Mark took an instinctive step closer to Aiden. "Aiden, what does that mean?"

Aiden's pulse hammered. "I don't know."

But Pecos did.

His fingers toyed with his coin again, flipping it absently. "They ain't people. Not like you and me."

Sarah swallowed. "Then what are they?"

Pecos sighed. "Weavers."

The word sat heavy in the air.

Aiden felt it in his bones—a truth spoken aloud that he had already known somewhere deep inside.

The gun in his pocket hummed faintly, like it recognized the presence before them.

The tallest Weaver tilted its head.

"You have taken something that does not belong."

Aiden's --. "I didn't steal anything."

"And yet the weave is frayed."

The air around the Weavers shimmered, as if reality itself was struggling to hold them in place.

Sarah's voice was sharp. "Aiden, we need to go. Now."

Blu took a step forward, his form glitching again, flickering between solid and something made of golden threads.

The Weaver's attention snapped to him.

Kyle's voice cracked. "Dude, tell me they don't see the dog—"

"Not yet stabilized. Anomalous."

Blu snarled, and the edges of his body blurred into something not-quite-animal anymore.

Aiden's grip tightened around the Destiny Gun in his jacket. His instincts screamed at him to do something—anything—

Then the Weaver moved.

Straight toward them.

Aiden didn't think.

He moved.

His hand tore the gun from his jacket. The moment his fingers gripped the handle, a surge of energy shot through him.

The Weaver lunged.

Aiden fired. No projectile—just a pulse that rewrote the hinge.

The gun didn't produce a bullet. It produced something else.

A pulse of golden energy rippled outward, spreading like light bending through water.

The Weavers froze mid-step.

For a single breath, everything in the park went silent.

And then—

The ley lines reacted.

The ground beneath them shook. The air fractured, splitting open like glass.

Reality tore for a single moment—and Aiden saw something beyond it.

A city that shouldn't exist. A sky made of woven threads. A sea of endless eyes, all staring back at him.

Then it snapped shut.

The Weavers were gone.

Aiden stood there, breathing hard, heart slamming against his ribs.

The gun was hot in his hand.

Kyle, Sarah, and Mark stared at him.

Mark finally spoke. "What the hell just happened?"

Aiden forced himself to steady his breathing. He looked down at the gun, then at the spot where the Weavers had stood.

Blu let out a slow, measured exhale.

Pecos broke the silence with a low chuckle. "Well, kid. You sure know how to make an entrance."

Aiden turned on him. "What the hell were those things?"

Pecos rolled his shoulders. "Weavers don't like when things get… messy. And you?" He gestured toward the golden rock, toward Blu, toward the air still shimmering where the Weavers had been. "You're making a real mess."

Aiden swallowed hard.

Sarah exhaled sharply. "Okay. No. We're not just walking away from this like everything's fine." She turned to Aiden, her eyes sharp. "You're going to tell us everything. Right now."

Kyle was still pale. "Dude. Those things weren't human. I don't—what even is this?"

Mark just watched Aiden closely. "…You already know, don't you?"

Aiden hesitated.

Then, slowly, he nodded. "Yeah."

Pecos smirked. "So. What's it gonna be, kid? You in?"

Aiden looked at his friends.

At Blu.

At the gun still humming in his grip.

Then he looked at Pecos.

And, finally, he made his choice. First step: map the seam they opened and find where it leads by dusk..

CHAPTER 4: AWAKENING

Aiden's hands still shook as he unlocked the front door and stepped inside. The night outside had felt charged, stretched too thin, as if reality had been pulled in a direction it was never meant to go. He wanted one thing now: to get everyone under a roof, to catch his breath, to understand the cost before it found them again.

Kyle, Sarah, and Mark followed in uneasy silence, their faces still pale from what they had witnessed in the park. Blu padded in last, but something was different about him. His golden-flecked eyes glowed faintly in the dim light, ears tracking a rhythm none of them could hear.

Aiden shut the door, pressed his back against it, and listened to the house settle—pipes ticking, air vent humming, the quiet scrape of Blu's nails on wood. The ordinary sounds didn't comfort him.

"What the hell was that?" Kyle burst out first.

Sarah crossed her arms, voice tight. "You saw them too. The things in the park. The… Weavers, right?"

Mark adjusted his glasses. "They weren't just illusions. They reacted to the gun."

Aiden barely heard them. His mind was spinning around one failure, one familiar weight.

FLASHBACK – THE COST OF HESITATION

The streetlights flickered as Aiden pedaled home, his heart still pounding from the Weavers, from Pecos, from the hairline crack in the ground that only he and Blu seemed to notice.

He had hesitated when they appeared. Froze long enough to feel the Destiny Gun turn heavy in his hand—long enough for something older than the world to look back.

Six years earlier…

The sun hung low in the sky, painting the streets in gold and amber. Aiden, younger and smaller, stood on the cracked pavement outside the corner store, gripping a comic in one hand and his allowance in the other.

Inside, two older boys laughed and shoved a kid named Lucas against a shelf, kicking his notebook across the tiles whenever he reached it. Aiden's stomach twisted.

He should do something.

His grandfather's words moved through him like a second pulse: "Hesitation is a choice too, Aiden. And sometimes, it costs more than action ever could."

Aiden stood there anyway, air caught in his chest. The moment stretched too long. Lucas hit the floor. A backpack dumped out. A sneaker flattened the notebook. One of the older boys glanced up, spotted Aiden through the glass, and tipped an imaginary hat.

They walked out. Aiden did nothing.

Present day…

The memory gripped him like a vice as he coasted the last block and threw his bike onto the porch. He had hesitated again tonight.

This time, the world had answered.

The Destiny Gun still felt warm at his side. Every time he touched it, it hummed—as if aware, as if keeping score.

Inside, something shifted in the air, a presence pressing against his thoughts. Then—a soft rustle from the far corner of his room.

Aiden's gaze snapped toward his terrarium.

The chameleon inside was moving, scales flashing erratically, colors stuttering from deep green to molten gold.

Mark followed his line of sight. "Uh… is that normal?"

Aiden's stomach tightened.

No.

FLASHBACK: THE ORIGIN OF SOBACCO

Aiden couldn't look away.

The chameleon's skin shimmered between hues that shouldn't exist—colors that felt like choices.

A memory opened.

Six years earlier—behind his grandfather's shop after rain.

Aiden—small, curious—spotted a chameleon half-hidden behind a soda can. Its skin was faded, its camouflage failing. He scooped it up and ran inside.

"You found a survivor," his grandfather said, laying out a cloth. The tiny creature pressed into Aiden's warm palm.

"Chameleons don't just hide," his grandfather went on. "They adapt. They mirror. Sometimes, they reflect things we don't even know about ourselves."

Aiden didn't understand then. He only knew he had found something special.

He named him Sobacco.

Present day

Aiden's breath hitched back in the here-and-now. The chameleon in the terrarium wasn't weak anymore. It pulsed with a force that didn't belong in a bedroom.

Blu let out a sharp whine, ears flattening. For a heartbeat, his outline fuzzed—edges not quite agreeing with the room.

Kyle took a step back. "Aiden? Why is your lizard… glowing?"

Mark, steady even now, said, "That's not a biological response. It's responding to something."

Aiden already knew what. Everything had changed when he fired the gun. When he tugged at the lines.

His fingers brushed the Destiny Gun's grip.

Sobacco shuddered.

A crack webbed across the terrarium—no impact, no strike—just pressure from something trying to be more than the space allowed. Golden fissures skittered along the glass.

Blu barked and leapt back as the terrarium shattered. Shards lifted and hung in the air, glittering, held by a pattern Aiden could feel along his teeth.

For one breath, the pieces listened.

Then they came together—not a tank, not a chameleon.

Something else.

The Transformation

The shards twisted into a taller, human shape. Gold-flecked skin flowed into muscle. Hair like Aiden's, threaded with metallic gleam. Eyes of molten gold found him without effort.

The new voice was his own, lower, steadier. "You wished for strength."

Aiden's breath stalled. This wasn't a mirror trick. It was a decision given body.

Kyle's voice cracked. "Oh hell no."

Sarah stayed fixed, skeptical and scared at once. "Aiden…?"

The figure tilted his head, reading Aiden like familiar pages. "I am what you asked for when you did nothing. The version that acts."

The Codex answered from the desk with a clean snap. Pages turned on their own and settled. Gold script bled into the fibers:

A reflection may guide or deceive. The path ahead is doubled.

Sarah frowned. "Meaning?"

Mark's eyes tracked the line. "He's not just a copy. He's a version. We don't know which way he'll pull."

Kyle gestured wildly between them. "We're not gonna pretend there are two Aidens in the room and that's fine?"

Blu stopped growling. He studied the newcomer—Sobacco—with the same careful look he gave thunder before it broke.

The First Conversation

Aiden steadied. "If you're me… what do you want?"

A flicker that might have been a smile. "To see if you'll carry the weight you fear."

"And if I don't?"

"Then I show you how to become more."

Sarah's gaze tightened. "Or he replaces you."

Aiden stiffened.

Sobacco didn't blink. "I won't replace him. I exist because he allowed me to. His actions created me. His choices define me. I am not his rival." He paused, head angling. "Nor his guarantee."

Blu's ears lifted a fraction, as if that distinction mattered.

The Codex breathed again, a soft lift of the page:

Test before you follow.

Mark's voice warmed with thought. "If he's tied to you, his existence depends on you choosing. Conflict won't erase one of you. It'll split your path."

Kyle groaned. "Great. Philosophy with consequences."

Aiden drew in a long breath. He didn't deny the fear. He reached anyway.

Sobacco extended his hand.

Aiden took it.

Heat moved through their palms, not a surge—just agreement. The Codex glowed:

The twin souls will forge a single road.

"What now?" Aiden asked.

"Now, we move," Sobacco said.

Kyle scrubbed a hand through his hair. "So we've got the original you, upgrade-you, a talking dog, a book that writes itself, and a gun that rewrites rocks. This is a group project from hell."

Sarah's arms stayed crossed. "How do we know he won't steer you off a cliff?"

Mark answered before Aiden could. "If he were the opposite, we'd be in a fight already."

Blu huffed and stepped beside Sobacco. For a blink, their gold flecks pulsed in time.

The front door eased on its hinges.

"Well, kid. You don't waste time, do you?"

Pecos filled the doorway, flicking a coin, eyes taking in Aiden, Sobacco, Blu, and the lit page without a single change in his pace.

"You knew about him?" Aiden asked.

"Didn't know when." Pecos pocketed the coin. "Knew it'd happen. You can't pull at the lines and not drag out what's tied to you."

Kyle threw his hands up. "Cowboy, clones, coin tricks. Awesome."

Sobacco watched Pecos without flinching. "You know the Destiny Gun."

"More than you'd think." Pecos stepped inside. "But that ain't your problem right this second. You're on borrowed time."

Aiden's stomach dipped. "Because I fired it."

"Because you announced yourself." Pecos nodded toward Sobacco. "Shadows listen. So do the ones outside the frame."

"The Weavers," Aiden said.

"And more than them. Keep that gun, the crowd gets bigger."

Aiden looked to Sobacco. "So what do we do?"

Pecos slid a folded scrap onto the desk. "You already know."

Aiden opened it. An address, neat and spare: 318 Kline Street — Rear Gate.

Under it, in a tighter hand: The Hibiscus Pact.

Pecos tipped his hat. "Time to see how deep the garden goes."

Aiden closed the note and met Sobacco's gaze.

"So, Gunbearer," Sobacco said evenly, "shall we walk this road together?"

Aiden didn't hesitate this time. "Yeah. Let's go."

*****

The morning sun found the school parking lot bright and loud. Students clustered by the bus; teachers counted heads; Mrs. Calloway waved a clipboard and preached marked paths and no restricted areas.

Aiden stood with his bag slung over one shoulder, trying to ignore the low thread of hum that hadn't left since the park. Blu sat at his feet—too quiet for a basset hound—eyes tracking currents through the crowd.

"Lighten up," Kyle said, clapping Aiden's shoulder. "It's just a garden. No monsters. Just plants."

Aiden forced a smile. "Yeah. Plants."

Sarah joined them, sharp as ever. "You two do realize 'just plants' is the last thing we saw before the park bent?"

"Let's not assume the worst," Mark offered. "We could have a normal day."

"Doubtful," Blu muttered.

The bus ride passed in chatter and glass-rattled turns. Aiden kept a hand over his bag, feeling the patient weight of the gun, the book warmer than it should be. He told himself it was precaution. Truth: he couldn't leave them.

The garden rose from its walls in green tiers—hibiscus hedges, shade trees, courtyards veined by gravel. The air smelled of sap and damp stone. Somewhere, a fountain kept time.

Hibiscus in deep red and sun-gold lined a side walk, petals heavy like they'd been listening all night. For a moment, the place soothed him.

"This is beautiful," Mark said, crouching by a bloom. "Hard to believe it's tucked in town."

Blu sniffed, ears swiveling. "Something's… patterned."

Laughter cut the quiet. Eric—smirking, careless—lifted something gold. Aiden's stomach fell through him.

The Destiny Gun.

"Eric," Aiden said, stepping in. "Put that down. It's not a toy."

"Relax, Kalel." Eric's finger found the trigger, bravado on his breath. "What's the worst that could happen?"

Aiden reached—

Eric fired.

A golden beam lit a hibiscus in a clean wash. The class gasped. The bush trembled, leaves growing too fast, curling like hands; flowers blew open, petals with a faint inner light. Eric stumbled, color draining.

"What the—"

"Give it," Aiden snapped, and ripped the gun free. Eric didn't argue.

He fired again—deliberate, away from people—into a dense thicket at the path's edge. The air crackled. The shrubs thinned and parted, revealing a narrow, winding trail that wasn't on any map, glowing faintly along its spine.

Blu's stance dropped. "The ley lines answered."

Mrs. Calloway's voice drifted from the main path, bright with rules. No one here was listening.

"We have to follow it," Aiden said, breath steadying as the seam settled under his feet.

"You can't be serious," Sarah said. "Do you ever stop to think we shouldn't?"

Kyle swallowed. "She's not wrong. What if this just opens more…"

"It's already open," Blu said. "Balance won't wait."

Aiden nodded. "We go."

They stepped onto the new trail. The air cooled, as if passing under a lid. Vines glimmered like poured metal. The hum thickened, organized.

The path ended in a sanctuary—plants moving as if tied to a heartbeat, light filtering in sheets. At the center: a cluster of hibiscus with blossoms like small suns.

As they neared, the flowers shifted. Shapes lifted from petals— humanoid, the suggestion of faces learned from wind.

Sobacco's voice, level at Aiden's shoulder: "You have stepped into something old. Be ready, Wielder. The garden remembers its name, and it will ask its price."

FLASHBACK: LEARNING TO WALK AS A HUMAN

Blu opened his eyes expecting fur and paws and familiar gravity. Instead, angles. Limbs too long. Ears not hanging right. No tail.

He tried to stand. New legs shook. Balance fled. Aiden reached to help; Blu snarled on instinct and startled himself with the sound—deeper, stranger. Fingers —he had fingers.

"Blu! It's okay." Aiden's voice cut through the static. Blu's glowing hands flexed, eyes stinging. Every instinct screamed to drop to all fours and run. The body would not obey.

Between what he had been and what he was becoming, he learned to breathe.

THE GROUND REMEMBERS

Aiden's hand was still clasped in Sobacco's when the soil underfoot trembled.

Blu's ears flattened. "Careful."

"What did you do?" Sarah whispered.

The Destiny Gun pulsed once against Aiden's side. The Sorcerer's Codex, resting against his leg, flipped open with a violent flutter. New words burned onto a page as if heat found them:

The twin souls awaken, and the past remembers.

White flooded Aiden's vision.

He stood in a city woven from living vines and luminous petals. Tall beings— hibiscus folk—moved along crystalline walkways, robes flowing like water. Their voices were music Aiden understood without learning.

"We were keepers," one said, gazing upward. "Until balance broke."

Thunder rolled. The vision wilted. Limbs stiffened. Minds dimmed. The bright civilization collapsed inward until only flowers remained, rooted and quiet, holding what they could not say.

The backyard snapped back around them—but larger. A stone arch stood where fence had been, its sides ribbed with hibiscus trunks grown and trained over years. The blooms along it breathed faint gold.

Sarah's voice shook. "What just happened?"

Blu looked from the arch to Aiden. "We disturbed something old."

Aiden swallowed and slid Pecos's scrap into his pocket, feeling the inked words like a weight: 318 Kline Street — Rear Gate. The Hibiscus Pact.

The garden had answered the address. Now it was waiting for theirs.

CHAPTER 5: THE GARDEN NEXUS AWAKENS

The address on Pecos's scrap was still damp at the fold from Aiden's palm: 318 Kline Street — Rear Gate. Under it, in a tighter hand, two words: The Hibiscus Pact.

They rolled past the public entrance of the botanical garden and kept going. At the corner, where the brick wall dipped for service vans, a narrow iron gate waited under a canopy of hibiscus—red and gold blooms bowed with their own weight. The posted sign read STAFF ONLY, but someone had scratched a small circle with a vertical line through its center into the paint near the latch. Aiden didn't know the symbol, but his skin did. It matched the pressure mark on Pecos's coin.

Mrs. Calloway counted heads at the bus door and sent groups toward the main path with a chirped reminder about staying on marked routes. Aiden fell in with Kyle, Sarah, Mark, and Blu, then let their cluster drift until the teacher's voice blended into fountain noise and bird chatter.

Blu stopped first. His ears tipped forward; the gold flecks in his eyes caught the light. Aiden followed his line of sight to the side gate.

"That's not the entrance," Sarah said, reading the sign. "It's a liability."

"It's the address," Aiden said quietly.

Kyle leaned to the latch, grinning. "Liabilities build character."

Mark pushed his glasses up. "We could get expelled."

Aiden slid the scrap from his pocket and held Pecos's handwriting beside the scarred paint. The paper and the gate were the same kind of old —edges softened by time, still refusing to tear. He felt the faintest hum through the iron, like a wire behind plaster.

Blu gave a single, soft whuff.

Aiden pressed the latch. It lifted without complaint.

They stepped into a service corridor of crushed shell and shaded light. On the public side, the garden sang about pollinators and signage. Back here, the air cooled. The paths narrowed. The smell shifted from floral to green—sap, wet stone, soil turned by careful hands.

The Sorcerer's Codex warmed in Aiden's bag as if it had been in sun. He didn't take it out. He didn't need to. The weight told him enough.

"Tell me we're not trespassing," Kyle whispered, which meant they were.

"We're following an address," Aiden said.

They turned once, twice. The corridor ended at a low arch of intertwined hibiscus trunks grown deliberately into a gate. Someone had trained them with patience and wire years ago; the bark bore neat scars where ties had been. In the center, where two thick stems crossed, the wood formed a knot the size of a fist—smooth, dark, polished by more than weather. The same circle-and-line was burned into its face, not carved: a brand, shallow but permanent.

Blu nosed the soil at the threshold and backed one pace, as if stepping onto a cold stream. The hairs along his neck lifted. Mark crouched and touched the gravel with two fingers. "Static," he said, surprised. "Like a sweater snap."

"It's not static," Sarah said softly. "It's... organized."

Aiden heard it then—the low, ordered thrum he'd felt in the shop when the gun first woke. Not loud. Not even sound. Something regular under hearing, like a metronome for the ground. The hibiscus leaves nearest the knot trembled though the air was still.

He palmed the knot; sap-cool grain under his skin. A hairline of light unzipped inside the trunks—no flare, just a measured beat finding his pulse. A thread-thin seam ran from the brand down the inside of the trunks and into the path, the way sap follows a cut. It traced the corridor back the way they'd come and forward beneath the arch, a clean filament no wider than a hair, pulsing once, twice, settling into a metric beat.

Kyle swore under his breath. "No way."

Sarah didn't move. Her eyes were on the line the way a navigator's eyes find north. "Pecos didn't give you a shortcut," she said. "He gave you a boundary."

"A seam," Mark said, more to himself than anyone. "A seam the garden learned to hold."

Blu looked up at Aiden. Not pleading. Waiting.

Aiden set his palm flat to the knot. The beat met his pulse and matched it, or made his pulse match it—he couldn't tell which. The bag at his hip grew heavier; the gun inside didn't heat, didn't glow, didn't do anything a weapon should. It simply agreed that this was the right place.

On the other side of the living gate lay ordinary paths and numbered beds and a docent telling a story to a circle of second graders about pollinators. Here, the ground remembered a job it had been given and never released.

Pecos's two words were not a title. They were a contract.

Aiden lifted his hand. The seam-light faded to an ember but did not disappear.

"We're not shortcutting," he said. "We're swearing in."

"And if the garden wants a price?" Sarah asked.

"It always does," Sobacco said from behind them, voice steady. He stepped into the shade beside Aiden, the gold in his eyes answering the seam's beat without strain. "Pay what you owe, or pay what it chooses."

Aiden nodded once. He drew a slow breath, checked the weight in his bag, and put his foot across the line.

The garden admitted him. The beat deepened. Somewhere past the arch, something ancient turned its face toward them, as if it had been listening for this exact footfall.

"Stay on the seam," Aiden said, and they went in.

The Garden Warps

The wind sifted through a canopy that shouldn't have been there, carrying a green, mineral scent. Inside the rear grounds, paths kinked at angles that didn't exist on the public map. Hibiscus trunks braided into colonnades; petals cast an amber wash over crushed shell. The familiar perimeter fence was gone — replaced by terraces of living stone and lantern-orbs that drifted at shoulder height, breathing in and out with the garden's quiet cadence.

Kyle whistled, stepping forward with an easy grin he didn't quite earn. "Dude, did you plant magic beans or something?" He reached toward a luminous vine. It recoiled slightly, like a startled animal.

Sarah folded her arms. "This isn't normal. Not even by our new standards."

Mark traced a spiral cut into a pillar. "These patterns look like ley line markers," he murmured. "Guides."

Blu stood a few feet ahead, unnervingly still, ears pricked, tail rigid. "It's not awake — it's attentive."

The ground answered him with a low vibration that climbed Aiden's shins. The Sorcerer's Codex in his bag began to hum. He yanked it free and flipped it open. The pages were blank—at first. Then ink seeped through, as if rising from a deeper sheet.

This place remembers. It knows the wielder has returned.

"Returned?" Aiden whispered.

The soil under Blu's paws pitched. Blu yelped, his outline stuttering at the edges. He dropped to a knee, breath stuttering, gold in his eyes brightening, then clouding.

"Blu!" Aiden lunged.

Blu's fingers dug into loam. "I can—hear something," he said through his teeth. "Old. Like whispers through root."

"We get him out," Aiden said.

He reached for Blu's arm—then the path moved.

Vines surged up, not wild but precise, spiraling around Aiden and Blu, encasing them in cool green. Vines cinched with a gloved precision; cold resin kissed his wrists as the path tilted like a slow tide. The others shouted, but their voices muffled, as if heard through soil. The lantern-orbs blurred to streaks.

The world went dark.

Warm, humid air. A scent of damp stone and nectar. Aiden's boots struck a floor that wasn't stone or wood—it flexed underfoot, alive with a faint current he felt through his soles.

Light bled in. They stood in a cavern woven with bioluminescent vines; flowers dripped glassy nectar from the ceiling, ringing soft when drops met the floor.

A chime sounded—clear, melodic. Vines parted at the far end of the chamber. Figures stepped into the light.

They weren't human. Tall, elegant shapes with bark-smooth skin and eyes lit from within. Limbs like trained branches, robes of layered leaves.

At their center, a being crowned in gold petals, presence steady as a trunk.

"You have reawakened a sanctuary that has slept for centuries," the crowned one said, voice layered and resonant.

Blu pushed himself upright beside Aiden, breathing evening out. "Who are you?" he asked, voice low but steady.

"I am Solflora, elder of the Hibiscus Keepers," the crowned one replied, inclining their head to the others. "We tend what runs beneath your world."

Kyle, Sarah, and Mark spilled in with a stagger of air and panic, catching themselves on a rib of root.

Kyle blinked. "Okay, uh, not what I was expecting."

Mark's eyes shone behind his lenses. "A completely unknown civilization," he breathed.

A smaller being edged forward, petals bright with curiosity. "Are you real?" they asked, touching the sleeve of Mark's hoodie with careful fingers.

Mark looked at his arm. "I… hope so."

Solflora's petal-crown rustled in what might have been amusement. "Forgive Thrynn. Curiosity is a trait of the young."

Another figure, broader and thorn-armed, stepped to Solflora's side. "He carries a tool of war," the warrior said, gaze on Aiden's bag. "Why have you brought it here?"

Aiden's hand hovered near the weight of the Destiny Gun. "I didn't mean to," he said. "I don't even know where 'here' is."

The warrior's eyes narrowed. "What makes you different from those who came before?"

A thin crack sounded from the chamber's far wall, like ice shifting.

The Tablet and a Name

Aiden turned toward the sound. A boulder half-swallowed by roots pulsed faintly with the same light as the Codex's ink. Fractures webbed its face, widening as if something inside was breathing.

"I've seen this before," Sobacco said, voice tight.

Kyle cocked an eyebrow. "You remember a glowing rock?"

"No," Sobacco answered, moving closer. "What comes after."

A chill threaded Aiden's spine. He reached out.

The stone let go; beneath, a tablet breathed with old light. One name kept burning: Alaric.

"Is that… a name?" Aiden asked.

Solflora's gaze dimmed. "It is the name of one who wielded the gun before you."

Blu's hackles raised. "There's power on it," he said. "Unfinished."

Sobacco's hand went to his temple. He flinched, eyes flashing gold, then a deeper red, then settling. "This place—this name—" He shook his head, jaw tight. "It's like I know it, but I don't."

The thorned warrior—Brackthorn—shifted weight, thorns whispering. "If you have already forgotten your own past," he said, "then the sanctuary was right to seal itself."

Aiden bristled. "What happened to Alaric?"

Solflora looked to the tablet. "The sanctuary remembers many arrivals," they said quietly. "Few departures. Alaric… did not leave whole."

Kyle made a strangled sound. Sarah's mouth thinned. Mark scribbled two words and then stopped, pen hovering: not whole.

The Sorcerer's Codex fluttered in Aiden's hands as if in a draft. New ink surfaced, letterforms rising like breath:

Those who wield do not write history. They rewrite it.

Sarah kept her distance from the book. "That's not ominous at all."

Aiden's throat worked. "If the Codex remembers Alaric, what does it remember about me?"

Solflora's petals shifted. "Books show what is written," they said. "But this place can show what was meant to be erased."

They lifted one hand and a vein of light ran along the chamber wall, folding into a brief vision no longer than a held breath: a city of flowers under an emerald sky; a council pleading; a wielder raising a golden gun; a shockwave unseaming streets into threads; petals becoming mere plants. The image closed like a book.

"We were the Keepers—scholars who mapped currents under your world," Solflora said. "When erasure came, we survived by changing shape. We became what the Codex did not think to remove."

Blu stared at the fading afterglow, eyes wet with reflected light. "We did this to you," he whispered—no lecture, no argument. Just the weight of a realized cost.

The chamber trembled—first like a breath caught, then like a chest deciding to cough. Vines cinched, lanterns dimmed. Aiden planted his feet. The gun in his bag felt heavier, as if the gravity in the room had been adjusted just for it.

"You're yanking load-bearing threads, kid," a familiar voice said, sliding out of the half-dark.

Pecos stood at the chamber's edge, coat hanging easy, eyes not. He did the coin trick—flip, catch, flip—but the sound of metal on skin felt wrong here, like a knife tapped against glassware.

"You again," Aiden said.

Blu's ears flattened. "How did you even get in—"

Pecos ignored it, gaze landing on the tablet. Something in his face tightened, almost a wince. "I was hoping you wouldn't dig that up just yet," he said. "Timing matters."

"Who was Alaric?" Sarah asked.

"A wielder," Pecos said. "Like him." He tipped his chin at Aiden. The smirk thinned. "He lost."

Aiden swallowed. Not gone. Not dead. Lost. "Lost how?"

Pecos flipped the coin, caught it, pocketed it. "Ask better questions," he said, nodding at the Codex. "And stop expecting a ledger to tell you about a bill that hasn't come due. Books show what's written. What happens when the story isn't finished?"

Kyle scrubbed a hand over his face. "I hate cryptic old guys, I hate being underground, and I hate that we're apparently rerunning someone else's disaster."

A high, glassy chime cracked through the chamber. Solflora's head turned sharply toward the tunnel mouth. "No," they said, almost to themselves.

Aiden felt the air go thin. The vines at the entrance flexed inward as if bracing.

Space folded just beyond the threshold, not like a door opening but like fabric pinched and drawn through a ring. Shadow threaded into a human height and held. A masked figure stepped through, their robes reading as black until they caught the chamber's light and revealed themselves as woven geometry.

The mask's seams were stitched in geometric thread—the same cold geometry that haloed the Weavers.

"You shouldn't be here," Solflora said.

The figure tilted their head. When they spoke, the voice carried layers, as if time itself were the chorus.

"The wielder is unfit."

The figure lifted a hand and pointed at Aiden.

"Surrender the gun," they said, "or we will take it."

CHAPTER 6: THE FIRST CONFLICT WITH THE UNSEEN

Aiden felt it before he saw it.

The air turned dense and electric, humming with something wrong. A ripple pulsed through the sanctuary and the glow-vines guttered, their light ticking faintly like a Geiger counter under the weight of whatever was coming.

Solflora's golden eyes narrowed. "No," she whispered. "Not now."

Reality tore.

Not a smooth gate but a raw seam ripped open, edges grinding like cracked glass. Figures stepped through, robes swallowing light, masks without faces. They did not walk so much as glide, heat-haze bending around them.

At their center stood the one whose mask bore etched, faintly glowing geometry braided beneath lacquer.

The Sentinel.

They raised a hand and the garden fell still. Even the plants withdrew.

"The wielder is unfit," the Sentinel said. The layered voice arrived from several angles at once.

Aiden's fingers curled around the Destiny Gun. "Yeah? And who are you to decide that?"

"We are the ones who maintain balance." A beat. Then, as if for the record: "The Unseen." A slight turn of the head toward the flanking masks. "Our Shadowbound." A brief, unbothered glance upward toward the canopy. "And when threads break beyond our reach, the Weavers remember and mend."

Blu's hackles rose. "I don't like this."

Sobacco slid one step closer, blade low, crimson gaze fixed. "Neither do I."

"The gun is not for you," the Sentinel said. "It is for those who understand its burden."

The weight in Aiden's palm changed—less metal, more intent.

Blu winced, voice tight. "Aiden, listen—your emotions are shifting. The gun isn't reacting. It's steering you."

Aiden's breath hitched.

"Surrender the gun," the Sentinel said, hand lifting, "or we will take it."

Five masks cut left and right, boots never touching stone, formation knifing into a V. Ley-light condensed along wrists and palms, hardening into glass-bright blades and bowstrings of humming filament.

The Sorcerer's Codex shuddered in Aiden's satchel.

From the shade, Pecos's dry murmur: "Choice time, kid—fight or run."

A Shadowbound lunged, tip aimed heart-high.

Aiden's body moved. His finger found the trigger.

For the first time in a real fight, he fired the Destiny Gun.

The shot unseamed the air; stone and light slid half a hand's width out of agreement, then snapped back wrong.

For a heartbeat, nothing moved.

Then the sanctuary flinched.

Golden vines recoiled like startled serpents. The floor shed its leaf-litter skin to show old stone beneath, sigils waking in the cracks. Mark's voice cut thin and precise: "Buried structure. This isn't just a garden."

The Sentinel cocked their head, not afraid—interested. "So. Just like the others."

The others.

Heat climbed Aiden's throat.

Blu coughed. "That wasn't just an attack," he rasped. "It echoed."

The Codex bucked in Aiden's hand, pages riffling until ink surfaced like breath:

Each shot exacts three tolls—Echo, Attention, Tax.

The Shadowbound glided to re-engage. The Sentinel's fingers twitched and they halted again, poised blades glittering.

"This is your last warning, Wielder," the adjudicator said. "The gun does not belong to you."

Aiden eased one breath. The gun hummed, wanting to be pulled again. He let the want pass through him and lowered the muzzle a fraction.

The Codex flashed a clean line in gold:

The Second Seal is weakening.

"The second seal?" he whispered.

Sarah's eyes snapped to him. "That's bad, right?"

The walls answered. Etched lines crawled, trading places like sliding type; the space around them peeled back in thin curls to show something older beneath.

"Not another dimension," Mark said, already mapping angles. "An old one. This is a buried ley line temple."

Kyle's grip on his own courage loosened audibly. "Cool-cool-cool. We can leave, right?"

"You cannot fight what you do not understand," the Sentinel said.

Another figure stepped from shimmer—not the dusty drifter but Pecos wearing ceremonial linen and shadow, edges blurred like a mirage trying to settle.

Kyle blinked. "Did he just—change outfits?"

"Aspect-Pecos," Blu muttered.

Pecos's mouth quirked. "Let's say the Nexus borrows faces. I'd rather not watch you repeat the last wielder's mistakes."

At "last wielder," Pecos's coin went hot in his palm. He didn't look at it.

"You speak of things you should not," the Sentinel said, the layered voice sharpening.

Sarah caught Aiden's wrist. "We don't know what happens if you fire again."

"And if that's another seal breaking…" Mark began.

The Sentinel's patience folded.

"Enough. You are unworthy. You will not hold the gun much longer."

A snap.

The Unseen attacked.

Ley-blades scissored. Air screamed where an arrow of light passed and left a hairline slit in space before it healed.

Blu body-checked Aiden out of a killing lane. "Right side—high blade!" he called.

A black edge carved through where Aiden's ribs had been. Cold motes bled from the cut stone instead of dust.

Brackthorn threw his thorned forearms into a block, catching a descending saber; sparks skittered. Solflora's vines snapped forward to bind, but the Sentinel merely inclined two fingers and the binding blackened from the knot outward like ink spilled through snow, strength siphoned into their stillness. Solflora staggered, petals dulling.

"They're absorbing ambient ley," Mark said. "They're turning the room against us."

Kyle yanked a metal placard from a post—HIBISCUS VAR. AURUM —then flung it on reflex. The next arrow met the sign mid-flight, grounded with a tinnitus-pop.

"That was not science," he panted, "but I'll take it."

A Shadowbound's blade sought Aiden again.

Sobacco was already inside the arc. Steel met filament, a flare of wrong light. He fought like he had practiced this exact line before—weight sequence perfect, advance without hesitation. For a blink Aiden saw a corridor of eyes, masks lining both sides, and Sobacco stepping forward into them with the same guard, the same breath.

"Sobacco—?" Aiden started.

No answer. The doppelganger moved on memory, not command.

Sarah's fear hardened into plan. "We can't outfight siphons—starve them. Kill the light." She snatched a fallen branch and smashed a glowing orb. "Dim them—now!"

Blu tore down two more. Mark hurled his jacket over a lantern cluster. The temple's glow ticked lower. The Shadowbound's edges dulled a shade.

The gun thrummed in Aiden's hand, delighted by the narrowing field. He almost—

He didn't. He let the current slide past his finger.

Hair rose along his arms without wind. Stone underfoot decided it didn't agree with itself anymore.

"Three radial cracks," Mark shouted, eyes wide behind lenses. "Converging—under—you—move!"

They did not move fast enough.

The Sanctuary Collapses into the Nexus Temple

Three cracks ran like second hands and met under Aiden's heel.

The floor let go.

They dropped through a skin of garden into cold architecture. The impact surprised warmth out of the stone—warmer than the air, not dead, not inert. Sigils woke in the walls, blue-white and old.

Kyle groaned. "Ow."

Sarah pushed to her feet, scanning the carvings. "What is this place?"

"An ancient ley temple," Mark breathed. "Older than the sanctuary. Buried for a reason."

The Unseen landed without a sound. The Sentinel stood on a ledge above, steady as a nail driven to the head.

The Codex screamed.

Pages flared and settled. New glyphs burned through the vellum, readable even across the aisle of panic:

The Second Seal is undone.
The past is no longer certain.
Seven seals. Two are waking.

For the first time since arriving, the Sentinel missed a step, balance shifting a fraction.

Kyle pointed, wild-eyed. "Did reality just—stutter?"

"The temple is tied to time," Mark said. "We unsealed something."

Blu's ears angled forward. "They're... stopping."

He was right. The Shadowbound lowered blades a breath. The Sentinel's hand fell to their side. Weight bled out of the room.

Aiden squinted up. "What are they waiting for?"

Pecos flipped his coin, silver flashing, then disappearing. "They got what they came for."

"They didn't take anything," Aiden snapped.

Pecos's look was almost kind. "Didn't they?"

The Sentinel turned toward the closing seam. When they spoke again, their voice wasn't layered. It was human and tired.

"This battle was never about the gun."

They stepped through. The Shadowbound followed. The portal zipped shut, seamless stone once more.

Silence.

*****

Dust hung. Aiden's knuckles blanched around the gun's grip.

Kyle sagged against a fallen block. "So—uh. We won?"

Sarah's glare said no. "That was a test."

Pecos chuckled without humor. "Could've gone worse."

"What just happened?" Aiden demanded.

"Something broke," Pecos said simply. His eyes flicked to the Codex. No smirk. "Things don't break without consequences."

The book still hummed. The words glowed stubborn and calm:

Wielders are levers; the fulcrum is what moves.

Blu pressed close, steady but tense. "The ley lines are agitated. Not here —elsewhere."

"Above ground?" Sarah asked.

"Far," Blu said. "Loud."

Sobacco stood apart, blade half-sheathed, gaze roaming the carvings. He hadn't waited for orders. He hadn't needed them. He looked like a man who had stepped into his own footprints.

A buzz cut the quiet.

Kyle looked at his phone. "Huh. Reception found us."

Aiden's stomach was already dropping. "What is it?"

Kyle swiped, blinked, paled, turned the screen.

A high-gloss flyer, trending hard: a stylized image of the Destiny Gun.

> The Ultimate Destiny Gun Experience — Unveiling the Truth Behind DG: Code Zero.
> Comic-Con.
> Today. Doors in four hours.

Blu's ears went flat. "That's the same gun."

Mark leaned closer. "No way that's a coincidence."

Sarah closed her eyes, then opened them sharper. "It's bait or it's a breach. Either way, we can't ignore it."

Aiden's hand wouldn't shake. He wouldn't let it. "We don't have tickets."

Pecos rolled the coin across his knuckles. "You have a seam."

Aiden swallowed once, set the gun's barrel down a breath, and looked at his friends.

"Then we go."

CHAPTER 7: THE GUN'S TRUTH & COMIC-CON CHAOS

Arrival at Comic-Con
Location: From the Nexus Temple to Comic-Con

The morning sunlight slid along the rideshare's tinted glass as the van merged onto Harbor Drive. The Convention Center gleamed ahead, banners snapping in the ocean breeze, armor-clad cosplayers moving like a tide along the sidewalks. The con's noise wasn't sound—it was want. A thousand tiny hopes brushing Aiden's skin.

He barely heard any of it. The Unseen's words still rang from the Nexus Temple.

This battle was never about the gun.

Blu sat shoulder-to-shoulder beside him, eyes unfixed, ears tilting as if he were listening to something beneath the asphalt. "The ley lines here are… off," he murmured. "Not chaotic like the temple, but—hidden."

"Underground?" Aiden asked.

Blu nodded once.

Pecos hadn't been lying. During con week, Harbor Drive sat on a shallow seam. The rideshare rolled like any other van, but the road's skin was thinner; scanners would see what the seam allowed—props, not weapons.

"Dude, this is insane," Kyle said from the front seat, face pressed to the window. "Look at those LEDs!" A helmet's visor across the street flickered. For a heartbeat, its cadence matched Aiden's pulse.

Sarah didn't look up from her phone. "After collapsing an ancient ley line temple, we're going to a convention." She sighed. "Great."

Mark's glasses caught the light. "It's not random. That 'Destiny Gun' exhibit exists for a reason."

"Someone out there knows too much," Aiden said.

The van eased to the curb. Heat and salt air rolled in. Costumes. Props. Oversized foam swords that looked a shade too real. As they moved with the crowd, the PA system crackled above the steps: "Welcome to Com—Wi —… Wielder Check-in begins at nine." The glitch vanished as quickly as it came.

Blu's expression tightened. "Something is definitely under this place," he said, nostrils flaring. "Like the garden, but braided tighter."

"Maybe it's an underground lair," Kyle grinned.

"Or another time-warping death trap," Sarah said dryly.

The glass doors swept open and the crowd carried them inside.

Location: Inside the Convention Hall

Bright neon signage; banners three stories tall; animatronic suits whirring. The floor thrummed with footfalls and unspent adrenaline. Aiden felt the shift immediately—like standing in a field before a storm.

"THIS. IS. AMAZING," Kyle announced to no one in particular.

"We should split up," Mark said, scanning the booths. "Look for anything that connects to the Nexus Temple."

Aiden didn't move. A massive screen over a central aisle blinked to a new ad:

EXPERIENCE THE DESTINY GUN: THE TRUTH BEHIND DG: CODE ZERO EXCLUSIVE UNDERGROUND EXHIBIT – LIMITED ENTRY

His stomach tightened.

Sarah read over his shoulder. "We found it."

Blu's jaw set. "No. It found us."

Entering the DG: Code Zero Exhibit
Location: From the Convention Hall
to the Underground Level

The booth hid in plain sight between two franchise monoliths. Minimalist. Black. A holographic Destiny Gun rotated in patient silence above a sleek entry panel.

Aiden's pulse jumped.

The attendant—a woman in a crisp, not-quite-uniform—glanced up. Her look was professionally neutral, but her eyes recognized them. "Welcome. DG: Code Zero?"

"…Yeah," Aiden said.

Her gaze clipped over the Codex's strap on his shoulder, then down. She lifted a compact console; a red beam arced toward their badges. The scanner chirped green before the beam touched plastic.

Sarah frowned. "It lit up early," she whispered.

"VIP access confirmed," the attendant said, already stepping aside.

"Since when do we—" Sarah began, but the wall slid open with a sealed hush, revealing a narrow black stair.

Kyle nearly bounced. "Oh, this is so freaking cool."

Blu muttered, "This is the worst idea," but followed anyway.

The door sealed behind them. The stairwell smelled faintly of ozone and metal.

Location: The Underground Exhibit —

The Destiny Gun's Past

A corridor unfolded into curated darkness. Glass panels displayed faded documents, engraved schematics, a case of layered blueprints. Soft light made everything look like found truth.

"Where did they get this?" Mark breathed.

Sarah pointed at parchment under glass. "Centuries old," she said—and even she sounded unsure.

Kyle stopped at a digital console. "This one says the gun was part of a classified project?"

Aiden's hand drifted toward the Codex. None of this should outstrip a living book.

Blu stiffened. "There," he said.

At the hall's end, a solitary case glowed. Inside, a gun waited—identical down to every carved seam and whispering line.

Aiden's breath skidded. "That's… impossible."

"How the hell do they have a second one?" Sarah demanded.

Blu stepped closer, then flattened his ears. "No. This isn't the same." He inhaled again, as if scent might exist for an idea. "It's… a shadow."

The Codex warmed against Aiden's palm. Not forged—reflected.

The display's screen flickered above the case. Static formed a figure in scarred armor, face fogged by the transmission. A burden sagged his stance; the outline of the Destiny Gun rode his back like a verdict.

"The gun was never meant to be fired," the projection said. "Yet here you stand."

Aiden's lungs forgot their job. Blu's voice thinned: "This just got worse."

First Encounter with the Pen Wizards

Wind lifted at the corridor's far end where no vents existed. A heat-scent, sharp as singed paper, threaded the air. Five figures slid out of shadow like the ink of their own signatures.

Cosplay would've recognized them as elemental chic. Nothing about them was costume.

"You shouldn't be here," their leader said. Her gown was a crimson geography of flames stitched in thread the color of molten gold. Her eyes kept their own embers.

Aiden raised empty hands. "I could say the same."

Kyle leaned toward Sarah. "Are we about to have a wizard duel? Because that would be—"

"—a terrible idea," Sarah finished. "Who are you?"

The woman lifted a pen—a quill of obsidian lacquer with a ruby-lit tip. Power licked off it like heat off asphalt. "We are the Pen Wizards of Tertio Regni," she said. "And you are disrupting the balance of the ley lines."

Blu set a paw-hand to the floor, shoulders ready. "Funny," he said evenly. "We were thinking the same about you."

They fanned to a practiced formation:

> Liora: Fire - flame annotating the air like margin notes written in heat.
> Caius: Earth - broad, patient, stance like bedrock.
> Selene: Water - ice hem glittered frost; her breath drew patterns on air.
> Aeryn: Wind - cloak tugged by a breeze that belonged only to him.
> Mara: Shadow - violet-black, edges untrusted by light.

"We're not here to fight," Aiden said.

"Then explain why your gun distorts reality," Liora shot back.

"You… know about it?" Aiden asked.

Selene's eyes were winter-clear. "It's warping the lines. We can feel it."

"If you won't surrender the weapon," Liora said, "we'll take it and close the breach you carry."

The ground answered her threat. Stone erupted in a jagged wall between Aiden's team.

Caius moved like a landslide. Blu was faster—his claws split the first barrier, but the next rose to replace it. Aeryn's pen traced a green glyph; wind howled down the corridor. Ice spilled underfoot in a slick Selene wave. Aiden skidded, catching himself on the case.

Kyle pinwheeled and grabbed Mark. "I knew Comic-Con would end in a boss battle!"

"Move," Sarah snapped, flipping the Codex open. Pages glowed like a kiln set to low.

Liora advanced, her flame coiling up the quill. "Your weapon doesn't belong here. The lines can't take it."

"We're trying to fix this," Aiden said—and meant it.

Mara stepped once. Shadows slipped around her ankles like willing dogs. "Then prove it."

"Hold your ground!" Blu barked, launching at Aeryn. Claws met wind-sigils with a crack of air.

Sarah's fingers flew. "Ley-line balance—patterns—intent," she murmured, then found it. "They're reacting to focus," she said. "If we direct our intent, we can counter the surge."

"In normal language?" Kyle groaned from the ice.

Mark shoved him upright. "Fight creatively."

Aiden lifted the Gun—not to fire. To aim the hum. He let the pressure in his palm widen like breath, then thought not of attack but alignment. Golden resonance rippled out, ink blooming in water.

The weather in the hall changed.

Selene's frost stopped spreading.
Aeryn's gale settled, breath becoming breeze.
Liora's pen-flame flickered, annotating without burning.

They hesitated.

"See?" Aiden said. "We're not enemies."

"Remains to be seen," Liora said, lowering the quill a fraction.

Then Mara moved like an afterthought.

Her shadow slid under Aiden's grip and the Gun went quiet—terrifyingly quiet, as if someone had removed the idea of a heartbeat. Panic kicked his ribs. The Codex thudded against his chest; text flared, gold on gold, and the hum returned like air after water. Aiden's knees almost buckled with the relief.

Mara's eyes flickered, curious. "Better," she said softly.

Liora's flame drew a single downstroke in air and vanished. "If your claim is true," she said, "then explain why the lines answer you."

Aiden didn't look away. "Because this place isn't just on a seam. It's full of belief."

The Codex's Hidden Message
Location: The Exhibit's Inner Chamber

They stepped into the next gallery, a circle of panels around a central plinth. The room hummed—not with ley lines, but with people. Above them, thousands of attendees poured their excitement into the air like static.

"It's shifting," Blu whispered. His ears tilted toward the ceiling.

"It's not the lines," Liora said, watching as a holographic overlay glitched, then brightened. "It's people."

"Uh," Kyle said. "Guys?"

He stood before a metallic mural: a stylized wielder holding the Gun, ringed by shadowed figures—some kneeling, some reaching, some recoiling. Below, glyphic script curved like a verdict.

"The wielder does not command the Nexus," Mark read quietly. "The Nexus flows through those who believe."

Sarah frowned. "That's not ley line logic."

"It's narrative logic," Mark said. "The exhibit isn't just history—it's about perception."

A second panel showed another wielder. The poses matched. The crowd didn't. In one, worship; in the other, fear. The Gun itself looked older in one, sharper in the other, as if belief had filed or smoothed its edges.

"It's not the gun that shapes the world," Aiden said. "It's the way people understand it."

"And this entire convention is feeding that understanding," Blu said.

The room acknowledged the thought; the lights dimmed a shade, then rose.

"So," Kyle said, backing up, "we're in a focus-group for reality."

Sarah tapped the glyphs again. "It doesn't make power," she said, eyes on Aiden. "It leans the outcome. Bias, not creation."

A final panel waited at the far curve of the room. A fractured world, its edges splintering. At the center, a wielder faded into the cracks.

Mark read the last line. "A world with too many truths will lose itself."

The exhibit lights flickered.

The Gun pulsed against Aiden's palm.

"If someone wants you to be a villain—" Sarah began.

The room went dark.

A voice, laced with static, threaded the speakers. "Welcome, Destiny Wielder."

Aiden's skin crawled. The exhibit had not just found him; it had been expecting him.

Location: From the Main Hall to

the Hidden Security Room

A seam in the back wall whispered open. No hinge. No latch. Just a decision the room made on their behalf.

"We triggered something," Blu said. Every hair along his spine stood up.

"My phone's dead," Kyle said, tapping a black screen. "No signal. No nothing."

"We need to know who's running this," Aiden said, and stepped through.

Location: The Hidden Security Room

Cold air. Metal filing cabinets. Old monitors sleeping in stacks. Crates stamped with a split-eye sigil. The emblem wasn't paint; it was a thin metal wafer riveted to each crate, a faint coil-whine singing under the metal like a held note. The split eye hummed at a pitch only nerves could hear.

"No guards," Sarah said.

"Recently used," Blu added, running a palm over a dustless ring where a mug had been.

Kyle slid into a cracked chair and rattled the keyboard. The terminal wanted a passcode. "Plan B," he said to Sobacco. "Punch?"

Sobacco crossed his arms.

Aiden lifted the Codex. The book shivered in his hands; its pages ticked like a clock finding the right tooth. He held it near the terminal.

The screen spasmed, then calmed.

ACCESS GRANTED. WELCOME, WIELDER.

A folder tree rolled down. The top directory read: THE CONVERGENCE INITIATIVE.

"What the hell is that?" Sarah whispered.

"A funding body," Mark said, already clicking deeper. "Or a doctrine. Or both."

Aiden's jaw tightened. The name felt like a word someone had erased and then wrote again, harder.

Blu stared at the Codex. Its pages weren't just reacting; the text pricked and rearranged in sympathetic rhythm to the screen. "It's not just reading," he said slowly. "It's rewriting what was seeded here."

The temperature slipped. Aiden's vision narrowed, tunneled. His balance ticked in and out.

The lights went out.

A hologram rose from the console in a pillar of glitch-light.

Armor. Wear. A face mostly lost to static. The Gun on his back like gravity. The room seemed smaller around him.

"Alaric," Blu breathed.

Aiden couldn't swallow. The name had glowed under stone in the garden. Now it spoke.

"You don't know what you're carrying," Alaric said. The voice had the weight of someone who'd learned by losing parts of himself. The projection flickered; words pulsed out of order, staggered by interference.

"Those who wield do not write history—" the hologram said, then stuttered, as if refusing to complete the sentence.

"—you overwrite it," came through a beat later, warped, and somehow worse.

The room shuddered. The Codex snapped shut like it had been slapped.

Aiden's fear arrived honest and unhidden. This wasn't just his story. It was a loop. Alaric had stood where he stood. Alaric had fallen where he could fall.

"I think we just pulled on a thread bigger than us," Blu said.

"Then we find out why," Aiden answered, forcing his breathing to pace the Gun's hum instead of the other way around.

One icon remained on the terminal: ENCRYPTED_FINAL.codexlink.

"Manual decrypt," Mark said, already rolling his sleeves. "No Codex shortcut—if it's rewriting, we need a clean look."

Kyle cracked his knuckles. "Finally. Something I can break without breaking reality."

Footsteps passed somewhere beyond the wall. The PA upstairs burred back to life: "Code Zero Live Demo begins in twenty minutes in Hall D."

"Of course it does," Sarah said.

Blu's ears angled toward the ceiling, then toward the door. "Two guards at corridor bend," he said softly. "Not security. The cadence is wrong."

"Convergence," Liora said from the threshold. The Pen Wizards had followed in without fanfare; Mara's shadows settled like skirts. "We don't unmake tools," Liora added, eyes on Aiden, "but we keep them from rewriting the user."

"Then help us hold the line," Aiden said.

Liora glanced to her circle; they nodded. "Fifteen minutes," she said. "After that, whatever theater they've planned upstairs will harden belief around you."

"Bias, not creation," Sarah reminded, as much to herself as to Aiden. "We can still steer."

The split-eye sigils sang their quiet, nerve-level pitch. Aiden set his hands to the keys with Mark and Kyle, Blu at his shoulder, the Codex closed but warm as a warning.

Outside the locked room, the convention roared on as if nothing were happening. Inside, they began to pry open a file that had survived erasures no history book could remember.

CHAPTER 8:
CONVERGING THREADS

The hologram flickered, the battle-scarred figure of General Alaric distorting in and out of focus as though time itself were struggling to remember him. "You don't know what you're carrying."

Aiden couldn't look away. The Destiny Gun—his Destiny Gun—was holstered on Alaric's back, but the details were wrong. The engravings were different. Sarah's voice was tight. "This is recorded data, right? A pre-programmed message?"

Mark shook his head. "No. It's interactive AI. Look at the movement patterns—he's responding to us in real time."

Blu stepped closer, ears flattened. "It's not just reacting… it recognizes Aiden."

A shiver traced Aiden's spine. "How is that possible?"

The projection's voice warped. "You were never meant to wield the gun." The words rattled the consoles. It didn't feel like a warning; it felt like a correction.

Before Aiden could answer, the console beside him pulsed red:

SECURITY BREACH DETECTED. LOCKDOWN INITIATED.

"Ah, that can't be good," Kyle said, jerking upright.

The metal door slammed shut. Sarah spun to the monitor. "Someone triggered a security override."

Alaric's image glitched violently, froze—regret, or the echo of it, caught behind his visor—then bled away. A new voice slid into the room, calm and measured. "I see you found our little archive."

Mark's fingers flew across the keys. "I don't like this."

"Who are you?" Sarah demanded.

"I am merely an observer," the voice replied. "You may call me… Halcyon."

Kyle mouthed the name. "Halcyon? What is this, a bad cyberpunk novel?"

Blu's golden eyes narrowed. "What do you want?"

"That's the wrong question, Guardian," Halcyon said, almost amused. "The real question is: what do you want?"

The sensation Aiden had been trying to ignore pressed in—the curated files, the artifacts, the way every corridor had shepherded them here. "Why does the Codex keep updating?" he asked. "What is it trying to tell us?"

"That the world you think you live in is… incomplete."

"Concerning," Sarah muttered.

"So what, a loop? A simulation? An augmented reality experiment?" Kyle said. "Details, man."

"Details are for those who survive the first act."

Blu's fur bristled. "Who are you really?"

"We are The Convergence Initiative."

Silence held. The name fit the room like a key into an old lock.

"They funded this exhibit," Mark said quietly.

"Why us?" Aiden asked.

Halcyon hesitated. "Because you are walking the same path as those who came before you. And because if you keep going, you'll meet the same end."

A pulse rippled through the chamber. For a heartbeat, the walls turned thin as skin—shadows of past wielders flickering in the seams—then steadied.

"Run," Halcyon said, suddenly urgent. "I won't be able to hold them off for long. If you stay, you won't like what happens next."

Alarms screamed to life. The lock thunked open. Aiden looked to the screen once more.

"Find me before they do," Halcyon said. "I'll be waiting."

The connection died. "Move!" Aiden shouted.

Blu and Sobacco took point. They bolted into the hall as the chamber behind them shuddered, a faint coil-whine rising somewhere deep in the wiring; a crate by the door flashed a maintenance tag—H7F—before the panel went dark.

The hallway beyond wasn't the same corridor they'd entered. Dust hung in angled shafts of artificial light, and the pristine exhibit finish had given way to cold metal and forgotten bulkheads. Old holo-ads for DG: Code Zero hiccupped across the walls, half static, half ghost. Sarah rubbed her brow. "How does a convention hallway suddenly look like a decommissioned bunker?"

"No scent trails. No recent human activity," Blu said. "It's like this wing sits... outside the rest."

Aiden glanced back. The door they'd come through was simply gone. Sobacco's posture stayed blade-straight. "Someone led us here."

The corridor opened into a circular chamber beneath a domed ceiling. Obsidian flooring etched with pale geometry pulsed faintly underfoot. At the center, a glass cylinder held a relic weapon in stasis, rotating slowly.

Aiden's stomach dipped. It wasn't the Destiny Gun—but it was close. Sleeker. Older. Glyphs along its frame looked half-erased, as if someone had tried to unmake the record.

"That's not a replica," Blu said softly.

"Containment, not display," Mark added, studying the casing. "Stasis field. This was meant to be preserved… or buried."

This belonged to a wielder who'd been removed from history. Aiden didn't need the book to tell him. He stepped forward and brushed the glass.

The room bucked.

Ash and ozone replaced recirculated air. Sky tore itself into spirals; lightning feathered sideways across a broken horizon. Aiden staggered onto cracked ground littered with fallen metal and fractured sigils. In the haze, a lone figure stood—a battered visor, a blood-bound forearm, a gun that mirrored and did not mirror the one Aiden carried.

The figure turned as if he'd always known where Aiden would arrive. "You're late."

Aiden's mouth dried. "Who are you?"

"You already know," the wielder said. "Or you should."

Images knifed through Aiden's vision: the Destiny Gun, broken; a city subsumed by the Nexus; a stone sigil split in half; a name surfacing like a memory he was not supposed to keep.

Phelipandro.

The wielder's jaw tightened. "That name isn't meant to be remembered."

The battlefield cracked under Aiden's boots. Reality frayed. The man took one step closer, voice turning flint. "You're standing where you don't belong."

The ground dropped away. White ripped through the world. "Don't make the same mistake I did."

Aiden reeled back into the cylinder room, nearly collapsing. Blu caught him under the arm.

"Aiden! What happened?"

"I saw him," Aiden rasped. "A past wielder. He knew about the cycle. He knew about me." He swallowed. "Phelipandro."

Blu's body went tense. Kyle blinked, lost. "Okay, cool—what does that mean?"

"It means he was erased for a reason," Blu said, and there was fear in his voice.

A slow clap answered from the archway. Pecos lounged in the shadow there, coat worn, smirk easy—too easy. Aiden hadn't felt him arrive.

"How long have you been here?" Blu asked, stepping between them.

"Long enough to hear that name crawl back out of the cracks," Pecos said. His eyes cut to Aiden. "So, kid. How's that first sip of truth?"

"You knew," Aiden said. "About Phelipandro. About the wielders. About this... cycle. And you never said anything."

Kyle folded his arms. "Yeah. Convenient how you show up after the weirdest stuff."

Pecos chuckled. "You think I'm hoarding a grand revelation?" He leaned against a column. "News flash—I don't deal in straight answers."

"Don't or can't?" Aiden said.

The smile slipped a fraction. Sarah stepped in. "Who are you really?"

"We have records of past wielders," Blu said. "We have nothing on you."

"You kids make everything complicated," Pecos sighed.

"Then simplify it," Mark said.

Pecos rolled his shoulders. "Fine. You wanna know why I'm always around? Because I was curious. The Nexus doesn't care about timelines or cause and effect. It just… is. And me?" He gestured at himself. "I exist in that same gray."

Aiden felt cold settle under his skin. "You're Nexus-tied."

"Something like that," Pecos said.

"Was Phelipandro erased?" Aiden asked.

Pecos let the quiet stretch. "He was erased because he remembered too much."

"That doesn't make sense," Blu said.

"It does if you understand the cost of knowing." Pecos' voice went dry. "Phelipandro wasn't just another wielder. He was a disruption."

"A disruption to what?" Aiden asked.

"To the story."

Sarah's eyes widened. "Are you saying the actual history of the wielders was changed?"

"History isn't a straight road," Pecos said. "It's a tangle of choices. Sometimes people don't like where it's headed. So they rewrite it."

Kyle inhaled. "You're saying someone intentionally erased Phelipandro."

"Now you're getting it."

The realization settled like weight in Aiden's chest. The Destiny Gun's past wasn't forgotten; it had been removed. If Phelipandro was gone, who else had been?

"Why tell us now?" Blu asked.

Pecos looked only at Aiden. "Because you're the first wielder to start asking the right questions."

Aiden's grip tightened on the gun.

"You can keep digging," Pecos said, pushing off the column. "Chase ghosts. Unravel stories that were meant to stay buried." He turned toward the exit, hands in his pockets. "Or you can walk away."

"You know I won't," Aiden said.

"Didn't think so." Pecos took a few steps, then glanced back. "Just remember—there's a reason some people get erased."

He was gone.

The dim chamber hummed, geometry still breathing under the floor. No one spoke until Blu did. "What now?"

Aiden drew a steady breath. "Now we find who's been rewriting history."

CHAPTER 9: UNRAVELING THE CYCLE

The Convention's Artifacts Begin Reacting
Location: Comic-Con's Main Exhibition Hall

The buzz of excitement from the convention's crowd filled the massive exhibition hall as Aiden and his team moved cautiously through the crowd.

After the confrontation with the Pen Wizards and Pecos, the tension had barely begun to settle when Aiden noticed something strange happening around them.

The exhibits.

The Destiny Gun was activating them.

Sarah had her arms crossed, her eyes scanning the interactive booths surrounding them. "We need to lay low. We're being watched, and we don't know who's behind this yet."

Kyle, however, was fully engrossed in the energy of the event. "Lay low? Are you seeing this? I don't think we can lay low." He gestured around them, pointing at the massive fantasy weaponry displays, the sci-fi tech exhibits, and the replica relics from various fictional worlds.

Mark, ever the analyst, was already deep in thought. "If the Destiny Gun is affecting relics within the exhibit, then it means there's an underlying energy resonance happening here. We just need to figure out why now and why here."

Blu's ears flicked, his golden eyes narrowing as they passed by a large Atlantean ruins-themed display. "Aiden. Look."

Aiden followed his gaze—and his stomach tightened.

A massive sword, supposedly a prop from a well-known fantasy series, was suspended within a glass case. It was meant to be a mere convention display, a non-functional weapon used in filming. But the moment Aiden stepped within a few feet of it, the runes along its blade began to glow faintly.

For a split second, the text on the nearby information plaque changed, shifting from English into something unreadable—something ancient.

Then, just as quickly, it flickered back to normal.

Kyle blinked. "Whoa. Did anyone else see that?"

Sarah groaned. "Please tell me that was just a trick of the lighting."

Mark, however, had already pulled out his phone, scanning the text panel. "The digital display is glitching. It's rewriting itself in real time. But that's not possible unless—"

Blu tensed. "Unless the exhibit itself is being influenced."

Aiden took a step closer to the case.

The sword shuddered.

A sharp, faint hum filled the air, like a tuning fork in bone.

Then, a loud crack echoed through the chamber.

The glass began to splinter.

Aiden's breath caught.

The crowd reacted immediately—but not how Aiden expected. Instead of fear, instead of panic, there was cheering.

A nearby convention-goer laughed excitedly, pointing at the display. "Dude, this is insane! They really went all out this year!"

"That's gotta be pre-scripted!" someone else shouted. "No way that's real—right?"

Before he could speak, an overhead voice boomed.

"Whoa, folks! Looks like our special effects team is running their immersive exhibit event ahead of schedule!"

Aiden turned sharply.

The announcement had come from one of the convention's event coordinators, a woman dressed in a professional headset and badge standing near the main stage area. She grinned, clearly thinking this was part of the convention's planned entertainment.

A spotlight from above illuminated the sword case just as the glass cracked apart completely, sending fragments falling to the floor.

The sword inside tilted forward—but before it could fully fall, it froze midair.

Suspended.

Hanging in place as if held by invisible hands.

The crowd gasped.

Aiden's stomach lurched.

Because he could feel it—the same pull he felt with the Destiny Gun.

The sword was waiting. Reacting.

And it was looking for a wielder.

Blu moved fast. "Aiden—step back."

But before Aiden could react, someone else reached for the blade.

The Unexpected Challenger

A figure in a detailed knight cosplay—silver armor, flowing cape, and completely in character—stepped toward the suspended blade. Their hands reached for the sword with dramatic flair.

"This trial is mine to face!" they declared, completely convinced this was all part of the event.

The moment their fingers brushed the sword's hilt—

A sudden burst of energy surged outward.

Aiden barely managed to raise his arm against the force of it. The air rippled, distorting for a brief moment.

And then—

The cosplayer staggered backward.

Their armor flickered.

Aiden's breath caught. "No way."

Mark gasped. "Their costume—"

It was changing.

The convention-made, foam-and-fabric armor was solidifying, becoming something real—metal shifting, morphing, becoming an actual, functional set of battle-worn armor.

The crowd lost their minds.

"DUDE, THE TECH THIS YEAR IS INSANE!"

"HOW ARE THEY DOING THAT? IS IT HOLOGRAMS?!"

"THIS IS NEXT-LEVEL IMMERSIVE!"

The cosplayer looked down at themselves in shock, their fingers running along the now actual metal of their chestplate. Their eyes were wide, but not afraid—they were thrilled.

Blu growled under his breath. "This is bad."

Kyle's jaw dropped. "Bad?! This is incredible!"

Sarah grabbed Aiden's arm. "We need to go. Now."

Aiden barely had time to process before—

A second artifact began to react.

The Relics Start Awakening

All around the exhibition hall, small shifts started to occur.

A "replica" Atlantean staff in a glass case hummed with power, its crystalline core glowing faintly.

A display of ancient scrolls from a historical fantasy game rewrote themselves in real-time.

A full suit of Japanese samurai armor in another booth rattled, the shoulder plates trembling as if something inside it was stirring.

Aiden could feel it now—a ripple effect.

The Destiny Gun wasn't just interacting with relics. It was waking them up.

Blu swore under his breath. "This entire convention is a conduit."

Mark shook his head. "Not just a conduit—a catalyst. The Destiny Gun isn't just reacting to objects. The public's belief is making it stronger."

Sarah inhaled sharply. "Which means if we don't stop this soon—"

Kyle finished the sentence. "—Comic-Con is gonna turn into an actual battleground."

Aiden turned toward the sword-wielding cosplayer, still staring in awe at their transformed armor.

If the public believed something was real enough…

The Nexus made it real.

And right now?

The whole convention believed.

The overhead PA system crackled, and a voice—one Aiden recognized—came through:

"Congratulations, wielder. You've just passed the first test."

Aiden's blood ran cold.

It was the same masked figure who had left him the parchment.

Location: Comic-Con Main Exhibition Hall to

The Convention's Hidden Walkways

The convention hall buzzed with energy, a chaotic mix of excitement, confusion, and disbelief.

Aiden's heart pounded as the voice over the PA system faded.

"Congratulations, wielder. You've just passed the first test."

Every muscle in his body tensed.

That wasn't just an announcement.

It was a direct message—and it was meant for him.

Blu's ears flattened, his stance low and defensive. "Someone's tracking your movements."

Sarah grabbed Aiden's arm. "We need to leave—now."

Kyle, still reeling from the cosplayer's armor transformation, blinked. "Whoa, hold up—someone wanna explain how we're being tested?"

Mark, scanning the flickering digital signs around them, muttered, "That's what I'd like to know."

The displays were glitching, shifting between their intended convention schedules and something more cryptic.

Symbols. Coordinates. A single phrase repeating between panels:

Panel Room 7B – 10 Minutes.

Aiden exhaled sharply. "That's where we need to go."

Blu growled under his breath. "And what makes you think this isn't a trap?"

Aiden met his gaze. "It definitely is."

But they didn't have any other leads.

Aiden turned on his heel, pushing forward through the crowd. "Let's move."

Sarah, Mark, and Kyle followed immediately. Blu hesitated only a second before falling into step beside Aiden, his body language hyper-alert.

They weren't just walking into another mystery.

They were walking into a test they weren't sure they could pass.

Location: The Back Hallways of the Convention Center

Aiden and his team slipped away from the main exhibition hall, weaving into the hidden walkways typically reserved for staff and special guests.

The moment they stepped out of the public eye, the energy of the space shifted.

The hallways were dimmer, the buzz of the convention muffled behind thick doors. Aiden's footsteps echoed unnaturally against the polished floors.

Sarah frowned. "I don't like this. It's too quiet back here."

Blu sniffed the air, his golden eyes narrowing. "We're being followed."

Aiden glanced back. "You sure?"

Blu nodded. "Two… no, three people. Keeping their distance, but staying close enough to track us."

Kyle grinned. "Ooooh, are we being hunted? Because this is starting to feel like a spy thriller—"

Sarah smacked his arm. "Shut up and focus."

Mark was already scanning the hallway ahead. "Panel Room 7B should be up there, past the next turn."

Aiden inhaled deeply, steadying himself.

Whatever was waiting for them inside that room—whoever was testing him—was about to make their next move.

He wasn't ready.

But he had no choice.

Location: Panel Room 7B – The Invitation

The door to Panel Room 7B was slightly ajar.

Faint light spilled from inside, casting an elongated shadow along the hallway floor.

Blu growled. "This is a setup."

Aiden tightened his grip on the Destiny Gun, stepping forward first. "Stay close."

With a single push, he nudged the door fully open—and immediately stopped.

The room was empty.

No chairs. No stage. No panelists.

Just a single table in the center, and a folded parchment resting atop it.

Aiden's breath hitched.

Slowly, he stepped forward, feeling the air shift around him—like reality itself was paying attention.

Blu and the others fanned out cautiously, scanning the corners for hidden threats.

Aiden reached the table.

His fingers hesitated before picking up the parchment. The moment he touched it, he felt a faint pulse—a sensation that wasn't quite magic, but wasn't natural either.

He unfolded the note.

And read the words written in flawless calligraphy:

"The Destiny Gun does not belong here."
"Neither do you."
"Come alone if you want the truth."

A set of coordinates was written at the bottom.

Aiden's blood ran cold.

Sarah peered over his shoulder. "Yeah, I hate that."

Kyle squinted at the note. "'Come alone'? Yeah, no. That's a terrible idea."

Mark traced a finger over the parchment. "These coordinates... they're still inside the convention center."

Blu's ears flattened. "But in an area not open to the public."

Aiden swallowed hard.

This was it.

A direct invitation from the Convergence Initiative.

And they wanted him alone.

Sarah shook her head. "No. Absolutely not. You're not going by yourself."

Blu crossed his arms. "Agreed."

Aiden clenched his jaw. "I have to. This is the first real lead we've gotten—"

Sarah snatched the note from his hands. "And it's obviously a trap. They didn't even try to hide it!"

Aiden met her gaze. "Then why haven't they made a move yet?"

Sarah faltered.

Mark sighed. "He has a point. If they wanted to attack him, they've had plenty of chances."

Kyle crossed his arms. "Which means they don't want to kill him. They want to… what, recruit him?"

Blu exhaled sharply. "Or study him."

Aiden inhaled deeply. "I have to go."

Sarah glared. "Not alone."

Aiden met her gaze evenly. "I'll be careful."

Blu growled but relented. "At least take an earpiece so we can track you."

Aiden nodded.

Sarah, still frustrated, shoved the parchment back at him. "Fine. But if you're not back in thirty minutes, we're coming in after you."

Kyle smirked. "Oh, don't worry. We'll make it dramatic."

Aiden let out a small breath, appreciating the tension-breaker. Then, without another word, he turned toward the door.

His next steps would take him directly into the heart of the Convergence Initiative.

As Aiden left, Blu's fur bristled sharply, his eyes flicking toward the ceiling.

He could feel it.

They were being watched.

The Public's Belief Shapes Reality

Location: Comic-Con Main Stage –

Live Battle Reenactment

Aiden moved cautiously through the crowded halls, his mind racing with the implications of the Convergence Initiative's invitation. His team had split up momentarily—Sarah and Mark staying nearby to monitor him through the earpiece, Kyle wandering off (probably to grab a convention-exclusive item), and Blu tracking anyone following them.

His path toward the secret meeting point took him past the Comic-Con main stage, where a live-action battle performance for DG: Code Zero was about to begin.

The stage was massive, surrounded by holographic projections and fog machines, simulating an immersive battlefield. Cosplayers dressed as characters from the Destiny Gun universe prepared to act out a scripted fight between legendary wielders.

"Welcome to the FINAL SHOWDOWN!" the announcer boomed over the loudspeakers.

The crowd erupted in cheers.

Aiden barely gave it a second glance. He had bigger problems.

But then—

The Destiny Gun hummed in his grip.

Aiden stopped mid-step.

His fingers tightened around the grip as a sudden pulse of energy rippled outward, barely noticeable to the untrained eye.

Blu's voice crackled in his earpiece. "Aiden. I felt that. What did you just do?"

Aiden frowned. "I—I didn't do anything."

Blu's voice was sharp. "Then we have a problem."

Because at that very moment—

The battle onstage became real.

The Fight Becomes Reality

At first, it was subtle.

The actors performing the battle moved as expected, their choreographed attacks and dramatic dodges looking authentic. The props— foam swords, rubber knives, and plastic firearms—flashed with fake sparks and sound effects.

The crowd cheered, believing everything was going as planned.

But Aiden saw it.

A flicker in reality.

One of the blades—meant to be a harmless convention prop—glowed with real energy as it clashed against an opponent's weapon. The force of the impact sent one actor staggering back farther than they should have.

Another performer unleashed what was supposed to be a scripted magic attack—but instead of harmless pyrotechnics, actual energy surged forward, splitting the stage floor slightly.

The audience gasped—then applauded.

They thought it was special effects.

But it wasn't.

Aiden's heart pounded. The Destiny Gun was doing this.

It was feeding off the crowd's belief.

Kaida & Hiroshi

Before Aiden could react, two familiar figures joined the fight.

Kaida and Hiroshi—the Twin Dragons from the Revolutoh series—flipped onto the stage, their weapons drawn.

At first, Aiden thought they were just participating in the show.

But then Kaida swung her katana, aiming at one of the cosplayers.

The air shimmered, and her blade extended unnaturally, slicing through an opponent's weapon—cleaving it in half like paper.

The opponent stumbled back, eyes wide in shock.

The crowd lost it.

"OH MY GOD! THEY'RE USING ADVANCED TECH!"

"THIS LOOKS SO REAL!"

Hiroshi landed beside her, his daggers flickering with unnatural light. "Kaida—did you feel that?"

She nodded slowly, eyes scanning the stage. "Something's wrong."

Aiden took a step forward, calling out. "Kaida! Hiroshi! Get off the stage!"

But the fight had fully escalated now.

The actors weren't just performing anymore.

They were fighting for real.

And worst of all—they didn't realize it.

The Nexus Surge – The Illusion Breaks

Aiden knew he had to stop this.

But before he could move, the air vibrated again.

A heavy pressure filled the stage, like a low hum of static building toward a climax.

Then—

The entire set shimmered.

For a split second, reality overlapped itself.

The Comic-Con main stage—designed to resemble a sci-fi battleground —shifted into something else.

A real battlefield.

The walls became towering ruins.

The lights became sunlight breaking through smoke and debris.

The fog effects transformed into actual dust kicked up by shifting terrain.

It lasted only a moment.

Then it snapped back to normal.

The audience didn't even notice.

They thought it was another effect.

But Aiden saw the terror in the actors' eyes.

They had seen it too.

Aiden Intervenes

Aiden jumped onto the stage.

Kaida and Hiroshi immediately turned to face him.

"Aiden!" Hiroshi called. "Did you see that?!"

"Yeah," Aiden said. "And we need to stop it before it gets worse."

Kaida looked skeptical. "You're saying we're in actual danger?"

Before Aiden could answer—

A performer near the center of the stage panicked.

They had been using a prop gun, but the moment they tried to fire, the weapon shifted in their hands—becoming heavier, real.

And the next shot—

Was not blank.

The energy blast tore through the air, headed directly for the audience.

Aiden moved on instinct.

He raised the Destiny Gun.

The moment his fingers gripped the trigger, the entire room trembled.

The shot never landed.

A pulse of light exploded outward, absorbing the energy blast before it could strike the crowd. The bolt died against the field like rain on glass.

Everything froze.

For a moment—absolute silence.

Then—

The crowd cheered louder than ever.

"WHAT A SAVE! THAT WAS AWESOME!"

"BEST SPECIAL EFFECTS EVER!"

"THIS SHOW IS NEXT LEVEL!"

Aiden's breathing was ragged.

He slowly lowered the gun, looking at Kaida and Hiroshi.

They weren't cheering.

They were staring at him, horrified.

Because they knew.

That hadn't been special effects.

That had been real.

Security rushed onto the stage, but instead of shutting down the event, they simply acted like everything was normal. Their earpieces crackled in unison—"Ops to floor: treat as rehearsal. Keep the show moving."—and the smiles returned on cue.

The reality shift had already been dismissed by the crowd as part of the show.

Aiden felt sick.

Sarah and Mark appeared at the stage edge, urgently waving him down.

Blu's voice crackled through his earpiece.

"Aiden. Get out. Now."

Aiden turned away from the stage, moving quickly toward the exit with his team.

As he reached the backstage area, a figure stepped out of the shadows.

A man in a formal black suit, wearing a silver lapel pin shaped like a broken circle—the Convergence mark.

His eyes locked onto Aiden's, expression calm.

"Congratulations, wielder.

"You've just passed the second test."

Aiden froze.

The Convergence Initiative had found him.

The man reached into his coat, pulling out a sealed envelope, holding it out.

"It's time we had a real conversation."

Aiden stared.

He knew one thing for certain.

This test wasn't over.

Location: Comic-Con Backstage

Aiden stared at the envelope.

The man holding it was calm, patient, unreadable. His suit was perfectly pressed, his silver lapel pin—a broken circle—gleamed under the dim lighting of the backstage hallway.

Behind Aiden, the crowd continued to roar with excitement, completely unaware that reality had just fractured before their eyes.

Blu moved first, stepping protectively in front of Aiden. His golden eyes locked onto the man's, muscles tense and ready for a fight.

"Who are you?" Blu demanded.

The man gave a slight smile. "Someone who prefers discussions over conflict, Guardian." He extended the envelope a little further toward Aiden. "Take it. Read it. Decide for yourself if you're ready to listen."

Aiden hesitated. His fingers twitched near his holster, but he didn't draw the Destiny Gun.

Sarah and Mark caught up, panting slightly from weaving through the crowd.

Sarah immediately tensed at the sight of the suited man. "Aiden, who the hell is this?"

The man glanced at her, his expression polite. "Just a messenger."

Kyle, arriving a second later, grinned. "Oooooh, mysterious messenger guy. Love the vibe. Very 'secret society in a sci-fi movie' energy."

Mark's eyes narrowed. "That's because he is from a secret society."

Aiden finally took the envelope, his fingers brushing against the thick paper. The moment he touched it, a strange static pulse ran up his arm—not painful, but definitely unnatural.

He met the man's gaze. "What's inside?"

The man's polite expression didn't waver. "Instructions."

Blu growled under his breath. "You people don't give answers, do you?"

The man smirked. "Not for free."

Aiden broke the seal, pulling out a folded parchment. Inside was a single sentence written in elegant, inked script:

"To break the cycle, you must first see it for what it is."

And below it—

Panel Room 13C. Midnight. Alone.

Aiden's grip on the paper tightened.

Blu shook his head. "No. Absolutely not. You're not going alone."

The man in the suit chuckled. "I expected that reaction."

Sarah crossed her arms. "What do you people want with him?"

The man's gaze flicked back to Aiden. "To offer him a choice. No more, no less."

Aiden felt his pulse hammering in his ears. "What kind of choice?"

The man took a step back, hands clasped behind his back. "Come at midnight, and you'll find out."

Then—before anyone could stop him—

He turned and vanished into the crowd, slipping between attendees like a shadow fading into the background.

Aiden's entire body felt coiled with tension. He barely noticed the envelope crumbling slightly in his grip.

Sarah grabbed his arm. "This is a bad idea."

Mark pushed his glasses up. "It could be an ambush."

Kyle looked way too excited. "But it could also be the ultimate secret mission!"

Blu exhaled sharply, rubbing his temples. "We don't have enough information to trust them, Aiden."

Aiden exhaled slowly. He was fully aware of the risks.

But this was the first real lead he had about the cycle, the past wielders, and why history kept repeating itself.

And if there was a chance—even the smallest chance—that this meeting could give him answers?

He had to take it.

Location: Panel Room 13C

Hours later.

Midnight.

The main halls of the convention center had emptied significantly, though plenty of die-hard fans still lingered.

Aiden moved quietly, his boots soft against the carpeted floors as he approached Panel Room 13C.

His heart hammered in his chest.

Blu had argued against it for nearly an hour before finally relenting—on the condition that he and the others stay close, monitoring from a distance.

Aiden reached the door.

It was slightly ajar.

Aiden hesitated. Then, slowly, he pushed it open.

Inside—

A single chair sat at the center of an otherwise empty room. A holographic projection hummed in front of it, flickering with unstable energy.

Aiden stepped closer, his breath uneven.

The projection shifted, forming an image of a worn, battle-scarred figure.

Aiden's throat went dry.

It was the same mysterious wielder from his vision—Phelipandro. His image was distorted, as if it had been partially erased.

Then—the hologram spoke, its voice fragmented.

"You… should not be here."

Aiden's heart skipped a beat.

"The cycle is broken. You were not meant to exist."

The lights in the room flickered.

Aiden took a step forward. "Who erased you?"

The projection flickered violently.

"You do not understand… the cost of remembering."

"Some wielders vanish. Others become something worse."

Aiden's fists tightened. "What do you mean?"

Phelipandro's figure warped, voice becoming jagged.

"To break the cycle… one must be willing to sacrifice what came before."

Then, suddenly—

The projection cut out.

The room plunged into darkness.

Aiden's breath hitched.

And just as quickly, the lights snapped back on—

Revealing that the hologram was gone.

Aiden's chest rose and fell rapidly. His pulse thundered in his ears.

Then—

The door slammed shut behind him.

A voice, low and unfamiliar, whispered from the shadows.

"Now you see the truth.

Now choose."

Aiden spun around—

But the room was empty.

CHAPTER 10: THE DESTINY GUN & GENERAL ALARIC

The Hidden Vault & General Alaric
Location: Convention Center – Lower Exhibit Halls

The air was thicker down here, heavier than it should have been.

Aiden stepped carefully, his boots barely making a sound on the polished tile floor as he and his team moved deeper into the restricted archive storage beneath the convention center.

Kyle exhaled, his voice a mix of curiosity and unease. "I'm just saying, a hidden exhibit with no records, locked behind a door that isn't supposed to exist, is exactly how horror movies start."

Sarah shot him a glare. "Do you ever stop talking?"

Kyle grinned. "Would you rather I scream and panic?"

Blu, walking ahead, paused at a reinforced security door, running his claws along the etched metal surface. His golden eyes narrowed. "This door… it's old. Older than the building itself."

Mark stepped forward, adjusting his glasses as he inspected the markings. "That's impossible. This convention center was only built fifteen years ago."

Aiden, however, wasn't focused on the age of the door.

He felt the gun hum at his side—not like an alarm, not like a warning, but like a recognition.

As if the Destiny Gun knew exactly what was behind this door.

And it wanted to see it.

Hours earlier, before they'd ever set foot in the lower exhibit halls, Kyle's dreams had already started to slip out of his control.

The Watchers

Kyle's dreams were no longer his own.

He knew it the moment he opened his eyes to a place he had never seen before but instinctively recognized. A grand chamber stretched before him —tall, spiraling bookshelves wrapped around the room like the coils of an ancient beast, lined with tomes so old their spines crumbled at the edges. The air smelled of parchment, ink, and something else—something familiar but just out of reach.

A circular table sat at the room's center, covered in maps, celestial charts, and pages filled with shifting words that never settled on one form. Around it stood figures draped in long, hooded robes. Their faces were indistinct, flickering between shadows and sharp, angular features. Yet, Kyle felt no fear. If anything, he felt… expected.

One figure stepped forward, lowering his hood.

Kyle gasped.

He was staring at himself.

Not just any version of himself—this Kyle was older, more composed. He wore the same glasses but with a strange shimmer to them, as if they saw more than they should. His robes bore a golden emblem shaped like an unblinking eye.

Kyle somehow knew—without anyone saying a word—that this wasn't just a look-alike. This was him, years from now, if he accepted whatever the

Watchers were offering.

The Watcher Kyle studied him, brow furrowing as if confirming something. "You're still unaware."

Kyle took a step back, heart hammering. "Unaware of what?"

The Watcher sighed and placed a hand on the table. The maps and papers shifted, reforming into a single open book—The Sorcerer's Codex, but unlike the version Kyle had seen before. This one was different. Its pages were golden, the ink flowing like liquid starlight.

"This is what should be," the Watcher said, motioning to the text. Then he waved his hand over the book, and the ink twisted, blackening, erasing some words while others reshaped themselves into new sentences. "And this… is what has been rewritten."

Kyle leaned in, scanning the changing script. His stomach dropped.

His name was there. Not once, but many times.

Kyle of the Grand Library.
Kyle, the Keeper of Secrets.
Kyle, the One Who Chose to Forget.

He staggered back. "I—I don't understand."

The Watcher met his gaze, a flicker of something close to regret in his eyes. "You are not just a historian, Kyle. You are a Watcher."

Kyle shook his head. "No. No, that's impossible. I would remember something like that."

The Watcher gave him a sad smile. "Would you? If you were never meant to?"

Kyle opened his mouth to argue, but a whisper threaded through the air. The hooded figures around the table stirred, their bodies turning like the hands of a clock.

Something was watching them.

A shadow slithered across the farthest wall, coiling like ink spilling through water. The Watcher's face tensed.

"They've noticed you."

Before Kyle could ask who, the room began to shatter.

The bookshelves split apart, their pages unraveling into ribbons of light. The celestial charts on the table burned away, replaced with cracks in the very air. The hooded figures blurred, their voices distorting into echoes of warnings he couldn't understand.

And then, just as Kyle felt himself being pulled away, the Watcher stepped closer, gripping his arm. His voice, urgent and quiet, cut through the chaos.

"Not every version of you makes the right choice."

Kyle barely had time to process the words before he was yanked backward.

Kyle bolted upright in his bed, drenched in sweat, his breath coming in short gasps. The room was dark, the only sound the faint hum of the city outside. He clutched his head, feeling the dull throb of a headache that hadn't been there before.

It was just a dream.

Just a dream.

But then he looked at his desk—and his blood ran cold.

Scattered across his open notebook were sketches of the same maps from the Watchers' chamber, drawn in his own handwriting. At the center of the page, a single phrase was written over and over:

"Not every version of you makes the right choice."

Now, back in the humming dark beneath the convention center, Aiden placed his hand against the cold metal.

The response was instant.

The vault door shifted, not unlocking through conventional means, but phasing, shifting its texture like liquid metal before silently sliding open.

Beyond it, a dimly lit chamber stretched into the darkness, lined with rows of forgotten relics, sealed boxes, and broken artifacts.

Aiden swallowed. "Looks like we found our exhibit."

The Forgotten Room & The Sealed Memory

The chamber felt different—as if they had stepped outside of time itself.

Rows of dust-covered crates and artifact storage racks stretched into the distance. Some items were locked behind reinforced glass, while others were sealed in reinforced containers labeled "Historical Anomalies – Do Not Open."

Sarah ran her fingers over one of the labels, her voice skeptical. "'Historical Anomalies'? What does that even mean?"

Mark was already flipping through a nearby digitized catalog. "These records… they don't match any exhibit on file. It's like this storage room wasn't meant to be found."

Kyle whistled. "I hate how that makes me more curious."

Blu's ears flicked. He turned his head sharply. "There's something ahead. Something strong."

Aiden followed Blu's line of sight—and his stomach tightened.

At the far end of the chamber, a single vault door stood apart from the rest. Unlike the security doors outside, this one wasn't made of metal, but something older—something unnatural.

The surface of the door shimmered, like it was barely clinging to existence.

And carved across its center, in a language Aiden didn't recognize but somehow understood, was a name:

GENERAL ALARIC

Aiden's fingers tingled.

The Destiny Gun wanted to react.

Blu stepped forward cautiously. "Aiden… do you feel that?"

Aiden nodded, exhaling slowly. "Yeah. It's like… I'm supposed to open this."

Sarah crossed her arms. "And that's exactly why you shouldn't."

Mark frowned. "It's odd. This doesn't match the Order of Destiny's preservation methods. If this was one of their secured archives, it would have standard biometric locks. This… this is something else entirely."

Kyle tapped the unearthly material of the door. "Okay, so how do we open it?"

The moment he touched the surface, the entire vault reacted.

A pulse of energy rippled outward, sending a cold chill through the room.

And then—

The vault door began to dissolve.

Not break. Not shatter. Dissolve, like mist clearing from a mirror.

Behind it, a holographic memory projection ignited, flickering to life.

A man stood in the center of the image, dressed in battle-worn armor, his broad stance commanding but burdened.

His hair was short, streaked with lines of gray, and his eyes held the weight of a thousand choices.

Aiden knew, before the figure even spoke, who he was looking at.
"You don't belong here."

The memory of General Alaric locked eyes with him.

The others froze.

Sarah whispered, "This isn't just a recording."

Mark shook his head. "No. It's more than that. This… feels like something alive."

Blu took a cautious step forward. "It's aware of us."

Alaric's gaze shifted between them before settling back on Aiden. His voice was calm but weighted.
"You've come too far. I don't know who you are, but I know what you hold."

Aiden instinctively touched the Destiny Gun at his side. "You mean this?"

Alaric's image flickered, and for a split second, his expression changed.

It wasn't anger or recognition.

It was regret.

"That gun was never meant to be fired. Yet every wielder before you has tried."

Sarah whispered, "Tried what?"

Alaric exhaled, as if the memory itself carried the weight of history.
"To change the past. To break the cycle. To do what none before them could."
"And every single one of them failed."

The chamber grew colder.

Aiden swallowed, his heart pounding. "Failed how?"

Alaric's voice darkened.

"They either vanished... or became something worse."

The memory glitched violently, as if someone—something—was trying to erase it in real time.

Blu growled, stepping protectively toward Aiden. "Something's interfering."

Mark was already scanning the projection. "It's unstable. If we don't stabilize it, we'll lose whatever this message was supposed to tell us."

Aiden clenched his jaw, stepping forward. "Alaric! What do I need to know? How do I stop this?"

Alaric's gaze snapped back to him.

"The Seventh Seal was never meant to be opened."

Aiden's breath hitched. "The Seventh Seal?"

The term had been whispered before, hinted at in legends, but never explained.

"They will tell you to break it. Others will tell you to protect it."
"But if you truly want to survive..."

The projection glitched again.

Alaric's form flickered, and his next words were distorted, stretched, fragmented.

"You must choose... before you are chosen."

Chosen by who? The Order? The Nexus? Or the gun itself? The thought made Aiden's skin crawl.

Then—

The projection collapsed in on itself, shattering into fragments of light and static.

The room fell into absolute silence.

Sarah exhaled, her voice barely above a whisper. "What... the hell... was that?"

Aiden didn't have an answer.

But one thing was clear.

They had just uncovered something no wielder was ever meant to remember.

Mark stares at the vault remains and whispers, "Guys... we weren't the first ones to open this."

The Order's Hidden Records
Location: Convention Center –
Exhibit Archives, Restricted Section

The silence in the hidden vault chamber was suffocating.

Aiden's mind reeled, replaying General Alaric's fragmented warning over and over.

"The Seventh Seal was never meant to be opened."
"You must choose... before you are chosen."

The projection had glitched out, collapsing before they could get answers.

But one thing was certain—they had stumbled onto a hidden truth the Order never intended for them to find.

Blu broke the silence first, his tail flicking with irritation. "That wasn't just a warning. That was a final warning—like a message left behind for someone who was about to make the wrong choice."

Sarah crossed her arms. "The question is... what choice? What does the Seventh Seal actually do?"

Kyle, ever the optimist, raised a finger. "Maybe it's, like, the ultimate do not touch button?"

Mark, however, wasn't paying attention. He was focused on the shattered remains of the vault door.

"Guys," he murmured, adjusting his glasses, "I think we have a bigger problem."

Aiden turned toward him. "What is it?"

Mark ran a hand over the fragmented edges of the vault's remains. The door had dissolved, but there were faint engravings beneath the metal surface.

The problem?

Someone had already uncovered this before them.

"This vault," Mark continued, "wasn't just sealed. It was resealed."

The realization hit Aiden like a punch to the gut.

They weren't the first ones to find Alaric's message.

Someone else had been here long before them.

Uncovering the Order's Hidden Archives

Aiden took a deep breath. "If someone erased this vault from history, there has to be a record of it somewhere."

Sarah exhaled, nodding. "The Order keeps records of everything. Even things they don't want people to remember."

Kyle's grin returned. "Which means... it's time for a good old-fashioned break-in."

Mark adjusted his glasses. "Technically, it's research."

Blu sighed. "It's trespassing."

Sarah cracked her knuckles. "Semantics."

Aiden smirked. "Let's move."

Location: The Order's Restricted Archives

The team moved swiftly through the convention's underground pathways, heading toward the section of the exhibit halls dedicated to historical archives.

Unlike the interactive booths and cosplay-friendly displays upstairs, this section was quiet, lined with temperature-controlled storage rooms and private research areas.

Blu sniffed the air. "No guards. That's… weird."

Sarah scanned the hallway. "No security cameras either. We should be setting off alarms right now."

Mark frowned. "Almost like they expect no one to come down here."

Kyle whistled. "Wow. They really underestimate how much nerds love snooping through forbidden knowledge."

Aiden reached the sealed archive door, which was protected by an old biometric lock system.

Kyle grinned, pulling out his tablet and signal disruptor. "Give me thirty seconds."

Aiden raised an eyebrow. "Since when do you hack security systems?"

Kyle smirked. "You think those early access game betas get themselves?"

The lock clicked open in fifteen seconds.

"Okay, I'm both impressed and disturbed," Sarah muttered.

Aiden pushed open the door.

Inside was a cold, dimly lit room lined with historical records, digital logs, and sealed containment units.

And at the very center—

A single metal table with a locked black ledger.

Aiden felt the Destiny Gun pulse faintly.

This was it.

The Erased Wielders

Mark hurried to the console, typing quickly to access the Order's classified database.

Blu and Sarah moved to check the sealed documents, while Kyle casually flipped through an old book about past wielders.

Then—

Mark's eyes widened. "Guys. You need to see this."

Aiden walked over. "What is it?"

Mark pointed to the screen.

A list of names.

All of them listed as Destiny Gun wielders throughout history.

The problem?

Some of these names had been erased, rewritten, or completely blacked out.

Sarah's breath hitched. "They deleted past wielders from history?"

Mark nodded. "And not just that. Some wielders' records don't match. It's like… they were replaced."

"Replaced with what?"

Mark highlighted a specific entry, one that stood out among the rest.

> Name: General Alaric
> Status: Deceased
> Cause: Lost to the Cycle

Blu frowned. "'Lost to the Cycle'? That's not how history records deaths."

Mark scrolled further down. "It gets worse. Some wielders have this status—"

He clicked on another name.

> Name: Phelipandro
> Status: Missing
> Cause: Removed from Record

Sarah whispered. "That means… someone erased him after the records were written."

Kyle muttered, "This is next-level historical gaslighting."

Blu narrowed his eyes. "The Order didn't just keep history. They changed it."

Aiden's pulse pounded. He knew the Order had secrets.

But this?

They were actively rewriting reality.

Aiden moved toward the black ledger at the center of the room. It was locked, but when his fingers brushed the cover—

The Destiny Gun reacted.

The lock snapped open.

Inside was a single handwritten message.

It was old, written in a style that didn't match modern scripts.

And at the bottom, it was signed by someone Aiden had only just begun to understand.

> "If you're reading this, it means I failed."
> "Do not repeat my mistakes."
> —Phelipandro

The room felt smaller.

Aiden inhaled sharply.

Sarah, Kyle, Mark, and Blu leaned in, reading over his shoulder.

Kyle whispered, "Okay. Even I don't have a joke for that."

Blu exhaled. "It's proof. Proof that someone wanted us to find this."

Aiden turned the page—

But the next dozen pages were blank.

Sarah's voice was quiet. "Whatever Phelipandro tried to tell us… was erased."

Aiden closed the ledger, gripping it tightly.

"Then we find the missing pages."

The lights in the archive flickered, and the PA system crackled to life.

A voice—the same one that had spoken to Aiden before—echoed through the room.

"You've seen too much, wielder."
"Now let's see if you're ready to remember the rest."

A cold, hollow feeling opened behind Aiden's ribs.

Someone knew they were here.

And they were waiting.

Location: Convention Center –

Historical Guardian Myths Exhibit

The PA system crackled, the distorted voice fading into an eerie silence.

Aiden's grip on the black ledger tightened, the weight of Phelipandro's message pressing into his chest.

They weren't supposed to know the truth.

And now, someone was watching them.

Blu's ears flicked toward the ceiling, his golden eyes narrowing. "We need to move."

Sarah nodded. "Agreed. If we stay here, we're sitting targets."

Mark motioned toward the main exhibit hall. "There's another section of historical records just past the atrium. If the Order altered the Codex, there's a chance they left behind artifacts with the original information."

Kyle grinned. "Sweet, more snooping. Lead the way, my nerdy friend."

Aiden exhaled. "Alright. Let's go."

Arrival at the Guardian Myths Exhibit

The team moved swiftly, slipping through the side corridors that led toward the historical wing of the convention.

Unlike the high-tech, neon-lit areas of the main exhibits, this section was quieter, the dim lighting and museum-like displays giving it a sense of weighty history.

Ancient banners hung from the walls, each displaying the insignia of a past guardian order.

At the center of the hall stood a massive mural, depicting the legend of the Guardian Beasts—entities sworn to protect the wielders of the Destiny Gun.

Blu stopped dead in his tracks.

Aiden, Sarah, and the others took a few more steps before realizing he wasn't following.

Aiden turned. "Blu?"

Blu's tail flicked, his ears pinned back as he stared at the mural.

Aiden frowned, stepping closer. "What is it?"

Blu didn't respond.

He was frozen, his eyes locked onto a specific part of the artwork.

Sarah stepped beside him, following his gaze. "Wait… is that… you?"

Aiden's breath hitched.

At the edge of the mural, carved into the stone as if it had been there for centuries, was the image of a golden-eyed, wolf-like guardian.

Its form was nearly identical to Blu's.

But it wasn't just the appearance that sent chills through Aiden's spine.

It was the inscription beneath it.

"The Lost Guardian."

Blu's Memory Fractures

Blu stumbled backward, gripping the nearest railing for support.

His golden eyes widened in panic, as if something deep inside him had been shaken loose.

Aiden rushed forward, steadying him. "Hey, breathe. What's wrong?"

Blu's breathing was ragged, his fingers clutching his temple. "This—this isn't possible."

Kyle blinked. "Okay, I know Blu's whole 'silent brooding protector' thing is his vibe, but this is new."

Mark frowned. "Blu, do you recognize that guardian?"

Blu's --. "I don't know. But I—" He winced, shaking his head. "Something is… wrong. I shouldn't know this, but I do."

Aiden glanced back at the inscription. "What does 'The Lost Guardian' mean?"

Blu exhaled, his hands trembling slightly. "I… I don't remember."

Sarah hesitated. "Blu, what do you remember? About before you met Aiden?"

Blu was silent.

Then, finally— "Nothing."

Aiden felt a chill. "What?"

Blu ~ "I don't remember anything before being bound to you. Not where I came from. Not why I became like this."

Sarah and Mark exchanged a glance. "But you always knew about the Destiny Gun. You knew about wielders."

Blu nodded, his voice strained. "I knew the knowledge. But not the memories." His breathing was uneven. "And now… now I think something was taken from me."

Kyle's smile faded. "Okay. That's officially creepy."

Aiden swallowed hard. "Then we get it back."

The Ancient Guardian Script

Mark's gaze moved to the murals surrounding them. "Wait. If this is depicting an erased guardian, maybe the text around it will tell us more."

He pulled out his tablet, scanning the inscriptions surrounding Blu's image.

Sarah helped, carefully tracing the carved symbols. "It's an old dialect. Some of this was intentionally scratched out."

Kyle raised an eyebrow. "Because of course it was."

Aiden peered over their shoulders as Mark translated.

The text read:

> "A guardian once bound to a wielder, lost between cycles."
> "When the wielder was erased, so too was their protector."
> "Memory unmade. Purpose forgotten."

Blu stiffened.

Aiden's grip on the Destiny Gun tightened.

Kyle exhaled. "Soooo… Blu was supposed to be erased, but he wasn't?"

Sarah crossed her arms. "If that's true, then how did he survive?"

Mark frowned. "Maybe… because Aiden took up the Destiny Gun before the cycle could erase him."

Blu stared at the inscription. "If I was erased… does that mean my wielder was erased too?"

The weight of the question hung in the air.

Aiden's gut twisted.

Blu had been by his side from the start. But what if… what if he had been bound to someone else before him?

And what if that wielder was one of the names the Order erased?

A Shadow of the Past

The air shifted suddenly.

The light fixtures above flickered, casting long shadows across the exhibit hall.

Blu tensed, his ears flattening. "Something's coming."

Aiden instinctively reached for the Destiny Gun.

The shadows at the edge of the room twisted, forming the faint silhouette of a cloaked figure.

Not solid.

Not whole.

A fragment of something lost.

The voice that spoke was distorted, stretched, layered over itself.
"You should not be here, Guardian."

Blu staggered, his hands gripping his head as if in pain. "No. Not again —"

Aiden moved to his side, gripping his shoulder. "Blu! What's happening?!"

The figure's voice echoed, deep and hollow.

"The Wielder failed. The Guardian faded."
"You are not meant to exist."

The moment the words hit the air, Blu let out a pained growl, dropping to one knee.

Sarah and Kyle immediately rushed forward, but an unseen force held them back.

Blu gritted his teeth, fighting something unseen. "I… I won't disappear. Not again."

Aiden's heart pounded. "Blu, you're not alone! I'm right here!"

The shadowed figure flickered, its edges breaking apart like mist.

"Then remember. But be warned—memories carry weight."

A final pulse of energy radiated outward—

And then the figure was gone.

The room fell silent once more.

Blu stayed kneeling, panting heavily, sweat beading on his brow.

Aiden crouched beside him, gripping his arm. "Blu. Talk to me."

Blu's hands trembled, his golden eyes flickering between panic and realization.

Then, finally—

"I remember… a name." Aiden swallowed hard. "Whose?"

Blu's expression hardened.

"My first wielder."

Blu slowly looked up, his voice barely above a whisper.

"Phelipandro."

Location: Private Meeting Room –

Convention Center's Upper Level

Blu's voice echoed in Aiden's mind.

"I remember… a name."
"Phelipandro."

It wasn't just a name.

It was a connection. A fracture in erased history now resurfacing.

The group had barely recovered from Blu's revelation before they received an anonymous message through Aiden's communicator—a set of coordinates leading to a secured room on the upper levels of the convention center.

No explanation. No sender ID.

Just a location and a time.

Midnight.

A Mysterious Meeting

The room was dimly lit, lined with old bookshelves, as if part of a forgotten historical exhibit repurposed into a VIP meeting area.

Aiden, Blu, Sarah, Kyle, and Mark stepped inside cautiously, their senses on high alert.

Blu's golden eyes scanned the room. "This place... it feels different. Like it's not entirely here."

Aiden nodded. The air itself felt thick, like walking through unseen currents. The Nexus was active here, even if no one else seemed to notice.

At the far end of the room, standing near a dusty wooden table covered in ancient texts, was a lone figure dressed in a dark suit with a silver lapel pin—the Convergence Initiative's sigil.

The man turned slowly, his face calm, unreadable.

"Mr. Cross," he greeted smoothly. "You made it."

Aiden gritted his teeth. "Who are you?"

The man gave a small, polite smile. "A messenger."

Sarah scoffed. "You people love your cryptic titles."

Kyle nudged her. "To be fair, it is good branding."

The messenger gestured toward the table. "We have much to discuss. The truth about your Destiny Gun, about The Order of Destiny, and—most importantly—about Phelipandro."

Aiden's breath hitched.

He knew.

Blu tensed beside him. "How do you know about him?"

The messenger's expression didn't change. "Because his story is not finished."

The Sorcerer's Codex – Phelipandro's True Identity

The messenger lifted a thick, ancient tome from the table—one Aiden immediately recognized.

The Sorcerer's Codex.

Unlike the fragmented, rewritten Codex Aiden had seen before, this version looked untouched by time, the golden lettering across the cover glowing faintly.

Aiden's fingers itched toward it. "That's... the real thing?"

The messenger nodded. "Unaltered. Preserved within the Nexus."

Sarah frowned. "But the Codex doesn't contain absolute truth. Even the Order admits it's been rewritten over the centuries."

The messenger's eyes gleamed. "Correct. But not this version."

Blu stepped forward. "What does it say about Phelipandro?"

The messenger carefully flipped open the book, revealing an illustration of a lone figure standing at the center of the Nexus.

Aiden's pulse quickened.

It was him.

Not just any wielder.

The first wielder.
The first to hold the Destiny Gun.

The one who tried to fix what had already been broken.

"Phelipandro," the messenger began, "was not just a wielder. He was the first nexus-bound being to fuse himself to the Destiny Gun—a man turned into part of the fracture itself."

Aiden's stomach turned. "Wait—what do you mean nexus entity?"

The messenger turned the page.

"When the Cycle first fractured, when the Order began corrupting history, one man took up the gun—not to destroy, but to restore."

Kyle's eyes widened. "Restore?"

The messenger's gaze locked onto Aiden. "The Order was not always as it is now. It was once a noble cause, dedicated to preserving knowledge. But when they learned that history could be rewritten, they began erasing what didn't serve their purpose."

Mark's fingers twitched over his tablet. "You're saying... the Order didn't just alter history. They started deleting entire realities?"

"Exactly." The messenger tapped the Codex's page, revealing a list of names—wielders that no longer existed in any records.

Sarah's face paled. "They didn't just erase people... they erased their choices."

The messenger nodded. "Phelipandro saw what was happening. And he used the Destiny Gun to try and restore those who had been lost."

Aiden whispered, "And what happened to him?"

The messenger exhaled.

"He failed."

Aiden ~ "What do you mean he failed?"

The messenger flipped to another page.

It showed Phelipandro standing at the edge of a rift, his hand outstretched toward shadowy figures—the erased wielders.

"He fired the Destiny Gun not to erase, but to bring back what was lost."

"But in doing so, he became something else."

Kyle leaned forward. "Wait, wait, wait. You're saying he became a Nexus entity?"

The messenger closed the book. "When the cycle couldn't erase him, it made him part of the Nexus itself. He exists outside time, outside memory. Neither erased nor fully present."

Blu's breath hitched. "That's why I remember him."

Aiden's heart pounded.

That's why Phelipandro's name had been missing.

That's why Blu had no memory of his first wielder.

The Order hadn't just erased Phelipandro.

They had trapped him in the Nexus, ensuring no one could ever bring him back.

The messenger carefully closed the Codex and looked at Aiden.

"You have a choice, wielder. You can continue down this path, unraveling the truth, restoring what was lost..."

His gaze darkened.

"Or you can turn back. Because the closer you get to remembering, the closer you get to sharing Phelipandro's fate."

Silence hung in the room.

Sarah, Kyle, and Mark looked at Aiden.

Blu's fists tightened at his sides.

Aiden's pulse pounded in his ears.

He had always assumed the Destiny Gun was a weapon of destruction.

But Phelipandro had used it to restore.

And the Order had erased him for it.

Aiden looked the messenger in the eye. "If you're telling me this, it means you already know my answer."

The messenger studied him, then smiled slightly. "I do."

He slid a folded note across the table.

"Then take this. When the time comes, you'll know what to do."

The moment Aiden touched the paper, he felt a pulse of energy.
And in the back of his mind… for the first time… he heard a voice.

"Find me."

The voice of Phelipandro.

"The Forgotten Wielders"
Location: Underground Library,
Beneath the DG: Code Zero Exhibit

The underground archives smelled of dust and old ink, a stark contrast to the gleaming futuristic exhibits upstairs. The air was unnaturally still, like a place where even time hesitated to linger.

Aiden, Sarah, Kyle, Mark, and Blu moved cautiously through the dimly lit chamber, shelves towering around them.

Blu's ears flicked. "Something about this place… feels wrong."

Aiden ran a hand along one of the book spines, the texture old, worn. "If the Order erased wielders from history, this is where we find out why."

Kyle, scanning the shelves, frowned. "Okay, but question—why does Pecos always avoid this section?"

Sarah, who had been flipping through an old ledger, suddenly froze. "Guys… look at this."

She turned the book toward them, revealing a list of names.

Each one had a date of wielding… but no date of death.

Kyle raised an eyebrow. "What's so weird about—"

Then he noticed.

Some names had been erased entirely.

Mark leaned closer, adjusting his glasses. "It's a pattern. The Order isn't just deleting wielders. They're deleting their outcomes."

Blu's fur bristled. "Like they never existed at all."

Aiden's stomach tightened. He flipped through more pages, finding another section—one with final entries from wielders' personal journals.

The last one sent a chill through his spine:

"I was wrong. The gun is not a tool—it is a verdict."

Blu stepped closer, his voice low, cautious. "Someone is here."

Aiden turned sharply. "What?"

Blu's golden eyes scanned the darkness.
But when Aiden turned—there was nothing there.

The Codex in Aiden's satchel glitched for a brief moment, a new blank page erasing itself before his eyes.

And only one word remained.

"Nexus."

"The Relic that won't Respon"
Location: Museum Hall in the DG: Code Zero Exhibit –
Atlantean Relic Collection

Aiden stared at the dimly glowing stone tablet, something inside him twisting in recognition.

It wasn't reacting to the Destiny Gun.

It was rejecting it.

Sarah and Kyle exchanged glances. "Okay," Kyle said, "why is it glowing like a save point in a video game?"

Mark examined the tablet's inscriptions. "This is old Atlantean script… but it's incomplete."

Aiden exhaled, raising the Destiny Gun slightly. If it was connected to the Seals, it should at least—

Nothing.

No pulse. No reaction.

Blu narrowed his eyes. "Why doesn't the gun recognize it?"

Sarah ran her fingers over the engravings. "Maybe because this tablet isn't connected to the gun at all."

Kyle's eyebrows lifted. "Wait, are you saying—"

Pecos appeared suddenly, standing at the exhibit's edge, studying them with an amused look. "Now isn't that interesting?"

Aiden turned, narrowing his eyes. "What do you know about this?"

Pecos tilted his head. "Oh, I know plenty. But the better question is: Why isn't the gun enough for what you seek?"

Aiden stiffened.

Blu's tail flicked. "Enough with the riddles, Pecos."

Pecos grinned. "Have you ever considered the possibility that the Destiny Gun wasn't the first artifact made to alter history?"

Silence.

Mark glanced at the etching on the tablet's lower right corner. It depicted a dagger piercing through a ring of stars.

Sarah's breath hitched. "If the gun wasn't the first... then what was?"

Before Pecos could answer, the lights flickered, and the air shifted.
The Order of Destiny had arrived.

Location: Exhibit Hall, warped by

"The Order's" Manipulation

The moment the air shifted, everything changed.

The walls of the exhibit morphed, turning into a surreal battlefield. The lights overhead flickered, the artifacts around them shifting between different time periods.

Aiden gritted his teeth. "This isn't a ley line distortion. This is—"

"A test," a deep voice interrupted.

A hooded figure stepped forward, surrounded by three other Order operatives.

Their presence felt wrong, like they were forcing reality itself to bend.

Kyle cursed. "I liked this place better when it was just nerds in costumes."

Sarah took a defensive stance. "What do you want?"

The hooded figure ignored her, focusing entirely on Aiden.

"Do you know what happens to those who seek the truth, Wielder?"

Without warning, the space around them fractured, and suddenly—

Illusions of past wielders surrounded them.

Aiden's breath caught.

They were reliving the final moments of those who came before him.

One by one, he saw them:
A mirror image of Aiden himself, standing alone, facing the Seventh Seal.

The illusions shattered, and the Order left behind a single clue—a map leading to the next Nexus.

"Sobacco's Nightmare"
Location: Aiden's Mind –
The Space Between Reality and Memory

Aiden collapsed, gripping his head.

The moment the illusions shattered, his vision spiraled.

Then—

Darkness.

He stood in a strange, void-like space, the ground beneath him shifting like liquid.

Before him, a man stood in the distance, wearing flowing dark robes, the Destiny Gun holstered at his side.

Aiden knew who he was.
The man turned slowly, his eyes glowing with an eerie, otherworldly light.

But when he spoke, the words were fragmented, distorted, like echoes of multiple realities speaking at once.
"The Nexus… the dagger… the cycle is incomplete…"

Aiden tried to move closer, but his body refused to obey.

Phelipandro's gaze darkened.

"It's not the gun, Aiden. It's the choice."

Aiden gasped, suddenly waking up in the real world, Sarah shaking him.

Blu hovered over him, eyes sharp with concern. "You heard him, didn't you?"

Aiden nodded, his breath ragged.

Then he looked down—

And saw that the Codex had changed again.

A new page had written itself.
A warning from the First Wielder of the Dagger of Nexus.

Aiden, Sarah, and Kyle realize their mission has changed—this isn't just about the Seals anymore.

They are walking into a battle for history itself.

The Drowned Bation: General Alaric's Final Stand

Beneath the crushing depths of the Atlantic Ocean, hidden from time and history, lay the Drowned Bastion—a city of light and steel, a sanctuary where humans and Merfolk coexisted in uneasy harmony.

It was once a utopia. Now, it was a warzone.

Alaric sprinted across a crumbling bridgeway, his heavy boots clanking against the reinforced steel, a burst of plasma fire searing past his shoulder. He gritted his teeth, rolling behind a collapsed pillar just as a squad of deep-sea raiders breached the dome.

Behind him, Merfolk warriors—sleek and armored, their bodies adapted for both water and land combat—lashed out with hydro-pulse rifles and electrified harpoons, fighting back against the incoming force.

Ahead, a colossal leviathan, all serrated scales and bioluminescent eyes, rammed into one of the outer energy barriers, its monstrous jaws snapping at the city's last defense.

And above, just beyond the domed city, a fleet of advanced war-drones hovered in the abyss, their cold mechanical eyes scanning for weaknesses, their torpedo cannons preparing for a final strike.

Alaric had seen many battles. This was unlike any of them.

A Glimpse Through Reality

Alaric activated his wrist-bound interface, quickly scanning the ley line fluctuations that had been spiking erratically for the past hour. The disturbances were getting worse.

Somewhere, up above, across time and space, another Wielder was altering the ley lines.

And for the briefest moment—Alaric saw him.

It was as if the ocean parted before his eyes. A rift tore through reality, and in that flickering instant, he stood in two places at once.

Before him, beyond the chaos of the battle, a young man held the Destiny Gun.

Aiden.

Alaric's voice cut through the storm of shifting reality. "Wielder! Listen to me—"

Aiden's eyes widened in shock. "Who—? What—?"

The connection frayed.

Alaric's world snapped back into focus. The moment was gone.

Damn it. He had seconds, maybe minutes, to reach out again before the ley lines corrected themselves. He had to try—

A plasma round struck the ground beside him, sending him sprawling.

The Pirates of the Deep

Alaric rolled, bringing his arc-pulse revolver to bear. He fired—a charged bolt of energy slamming into a raider's chest, sending the armored pirate flying into the abyss.

A second raider lunged—a deep-sea mercenary clad in pressurized combat gear, wielding a harpoon cannon with a burning plasma tip.

Alaric dodged, narrowly avoiding the projectile before driving his combat knife into the raider's chestplate. The blade barely pierced the reinforced armor.

A burst of movement in the water—

A Merfolk warrior—Sirena—appeared in a swirl of bioluminescent ribbons. She wrapped her whip-like energy weapon around the pirate's neck, jerking it back with inhuman strength. The raider's oxygen tank ruptured, sending him into an uncontrollable thrash before sinking into the abyss.

Sirena hissed. "You're getting slow, General."

Alaric grunted. "And you're enjoying this too much."

Sirena's sharp-toothed grin was the only answer before she dove back into the fray.

Above them, the fleet of war-drones began their descent.

A War on Three Fronts

From his vantage point, Alaric could see the battle unfolding on three different fronts.

The Pirate Raiders, scavengers of the deep, were breaching the city's outer structures, fighting both Merfolk and human defenders for control of the stronghold.

The Deep-Sea Creatures, drawn by the chaos, were smashing into the barriers, eager to consume anything that moved.

The War-Drones, controlled by an unknown force, hovered ominously, their weapons primed to erase the city entirely.

If the Drowned Bastion fell, there would be no second chances.

The Last Transmission

Alaric ducked into a control chamber, his fingers flying across a holographic console. He needed to send one last message through the ley lines.

The disturbance was still fluctuating. He could see glimpses of Aiden—his grip on the Destiny Gun tightening, his expression filled with uncertainty.

Alaric took a breath and forced his way through the interference.

"Wielder—hear me!"

Aiden flinched, staring into the hologram as Alaric's image flickered in front of him.

"Who are you?" Aiden demanded.

"There's no time!" Alaric growled. "You're meddling with something beyond your understanding. The gun is part of a cycle. If you do not break it, you will fall like the rest of us!"

Aiden's eyes widened. "Like the rest of you?"

"Listen to me! The gun isn't just a weapon, it's a key! And you—"

BOOM.

The chamber exploded.

Alaric was thrown backward as the wall behind him collapsed. Water surged into the city, swallowing everything in its path.

Aiden's face blurred in the transmission, his voice lost in the static.

The last thing Alaric saw before the connection severed—was the war-drones piercing the city's dome, unleashing a blinding cascade of destruction.

Then—

Darkness.

*****

Alaric's lungs burned as he struggled against the crushing pressure of the water. His armor was failing, his weapons useless in the deep.

He could see the wreckage of the Drowned Bastion sinking around him, the glowing forms of Merfolk survivors fleeing into the trenches, pursued by monstrous shapes.

Somewhere above, the pirate fleet retreated, their mission complete.

Alaric clenched his jaw, reaching for the emergency beacon at his belt. He still had one last chance to—

A shadow passed overhead.

Something massive.

Something old.

A single, unblinking eye the size of a warship gazed down at him from the abyss.

Alaric's breath hitched.

The Deep had come to claim him.

*****

On the surface, Aiden stumbled backward as the hologram of General Alaric suddenly cut out, replaced by static.

"Pecos," Aiden whispered. "Did you see that?"

The gunslinger flipped his coin once, his expression unreadable. "I saw enough."

Sarah stepped forward. "Was that real? Was he... was he alive?"

Kyle swallowed. "If he was, he's probably dead now."

Mark frowned. "Or worse."

Aiden turned back to the flickering remnants of the hologram.

Somewhere, beneath the ocean, a battle still raged. A battle he wasn't meant to see.

And yet, for the briefest moment—General Alaric had reached through the veil of reality to warn him.

Aiden gripped the Destiny Gun tighter.

Alaric had been right.

The cycle was repeating.

And if they didn't break it—he would be next.

CHAPTER 11: THE ERASED WIELDERS

The List of Erased Wielders
Location: Underground Archive
Beneath the DG: Code Zero Exhibit

The chamber smelled of aged parchment, dust, and something colder—like time itself had abandoned this place.

Aiden stepped forward, his boots soft against the stone floor as he scanned the dimly lit room. This place should not exist, yet it was buried beneath one of the most elaborate convention exhibits in the world. They'd already slipped behind plenty of "staff only" doors this weekend, but this felt different—deeper than blueprints, deeper than permits, like the building had grown a secret all on its own.

Sarah brushed her fingers along the ancient metal bookshelves, her brows furrowed. "How the hell has no one found this before?"

Mark, who had already pulled up a holographic scan of the floor plan, shook his head. "Because it's not supposed to be here. The official schematics don't show anything below this level."

Blu, standing still at the entrance, narrowed his golden eyes. "This place is old." He sniffed the air. "Very old."

Kyle's grin widened. "Soooo, creepy secret libraries beneath a convention hall? This just made my top ten 'Best Places to Uncover Forbidden Knowledge' list."

Aiden ignored Kyle's enthusiasm and approached the large iron vault in the center of the room. It was sealed shut, but the surface of the door was unnatural, shimmering slightly as if resisting reality itself.

His fingers tingled.

The Destiny Gun pulsed at his side.

He glanced at Blu, who gave a small nod. "It recognizes something inside."

Aiden inhaled and placed his palm against the vault.

The moment he touched it—

The vault doors unlatched with a mechanical groan, unlocking layer by layer, gears twisting and metal folding apart.

Inside, a massive black tome rested on a pedestal. It was thick, bound in something that wasn't quite leather, its pages edged in deep crimson.

Mark adjusted his glasses. "That… looks ominous."

Kyle grinned. "Which means we're absolutely opening it."

Aiden lifted the cover, revealing pages covered in elegant, ancient script. The ink was dark and precise, as if written by someone determined never to be forgotten.

Sarah traced a line of text. "This isn't just a record of wielders… This is a ledger of every person who ever carried the Destiny Gun."

Aiden's heartbeat quickened as he flipped further.

Row after row of names, all listed by date of wielding… but some were crossed out, erased, or left incomplete.

Then he saw it.

A list of names that ended abruptly.

The Erased Wielders

Mark's face paled. "These names... they just stop. No cause of death. No record of succession. Just—gone."

Kyle exhaled. "Okay, I'm no historian, but even I know that's not how things work."

Sarah's fingers hovered over the faded ink. "They weren't just forgotten. They were removed."

Aiden clenched his jaw. He kept flipping through, searching for any clue.

Then—

A name stood out among the erased.

Phelipandro.

Blu staggered back, gripping the nearest bookshelf. His golden eyes went wide, his breath coming in short bursts.

Aiden immediately turned. "Blu?"

Blu's fingers trembled. He reached for the book as if his body instinctively recognized something buried in those pages.

"I... I know this name."

Silence fell over the room.

Mark and Sarah exchanged worried glances, while Kyle, for once, didn't make a joke.

Aiden's voice was low. "Blu, what do you mean?"

Blu swallowed hard, his hands gripping his temples. "I don't know. But I remember something. A feeling. A... place." His voice was strained. "I shouldn't remember. But I do."

Then—

The Codex in Aiden's satchel trembled.

Its pages flipped violently, as if responding to the name.

Aiden yanked it out, holding it up just as ink began reshaping itself across the open page.

A new line of text appeared.

"To hold the gun is to bear the weight of the past. But the past is not always meant to return."

Then—

The ledger book trembled.

The ink within shifted, moving like liquid.

Sarah gasped. "The names—Aiden, look!"

Aiden's heart stopped.

As they watched, the last line on the list bled and re-formed, ink crawling into new letters.

Aiden Cross.

For a heartbeat his name shone wet and dark before settling into the same aged crimson as the others.

His name had just appeared among the erased wielders.

Reality is Changing

Blu's breathing sharpened. "Something is rewriting the past."

Mark turned to Aiden. "You need to put the book down. Now."

Aiden's grip tightened. "No. This is proof. The Order isn't just hiding things. They're rewriting wielders—erasing them."

Sarah's voice was tight. "Yeah, and you just got added to the list. That's not exactly comforting."

Aiden's mind raced.

If the ledger was responding to him now, that meant someone or something was observing this moment in real time.

And they didn't like what he was learning.

Blu's ears flicked sharply. He turned toward the entrance. "We're not alone."

The room grew colder.

A voice—calm, measured, authoritative—echoed from the shadows.

"You should have never come here."

*****

Aiden spun, his hand instinctively reaching for the Destiny Gun.

From the darkness beyond the vault entrance, three figures emerged, cloaked in deep blue and silver robes.

Sarah tensed. "The Order."

At the center of the group, Hunter-General Cassius—the Order commander who'd already tried to steer Aiden off this path once—stepped forward, his steel-gray eyes locking onto Aiden.

Cassius's voice was even, deliberate. "You're playing a dangerous game, Wielder."

Aiden held his ground. "Funny. It doesn't feel like a game to me."

Cassius sighed, glancing toward the ledger still open in Aiden's hands. "You weren't supposed to see that."

Kyle scoffed. "Yeah, well, maybe you shouldn't keep your creepy secrets in creepy underground vaults."

Cassius ignored him. His gaze remained fixed on Aiden. "That book does not tell the full truth."

Aiden narrowed his eyes. "Then why did my name just appear on it?"

Cassius's jaw tightened slightly. "Because the moment you stepped on this path, you became part of the Cycle."

Sarah crossed her arms. "So what does that mean? That he's already doomed?"

Cassius's gaze didn't waver. "It means the Nexus is watching him now."

Blu growled lowly, stepping between Aiden and Cassius. "We're not running from you."

Cassius exhaled. "I never expected you to."

Then—his hand reached into his cloak.

Blu tensed, ready to strike, but Cassius only withdrew a small, silver data chip.

He held it out to Aiden. "If you truly want answers, then take it."

Aiden hesitated, then reached forward, plucking the chip from Cassius's grasp.

Cassius's expression remained unreadable. "You will have one chance to walk away before it's too late. I suggest you take it."

Then, without another word, he turned and disappeared back into the shadows, the other Order members vanishing with him.

Aiden stood still, his heart hammering in his chest.

In his left hand, he held the ledger of erased wielders.

In his right—the Order's chip, containing information they didn't want him to have.

And all he could hear was Phelipandro's whispered voice, echoing from the Codex.

"History does not repeat. It erases."

The Order's Offer

Location: A Hidden Office Within the Convention Center

The room was sterile, illuminated by the cold glow of digital displays and dim overhead lighting.

The transition from the dust-covered underground archive to this modern, controlled environment felt like stepping between two realities— one lost to time, the other meticulously curated.

Aiden clutched the data chip Cassius had given him, his pulse still racing from the encounter.

Blu stood at his side, his golden eyes sharp, restless, as if sensing something was off.

Sarah and Kyle exchanged wary glances while Mark tapped at a holographic interface, attempting to decrypt the data.

Mark sighed. "Whatever encryption this is, it's not standard."

Kyle folded his arms. "Okay, so, just a quick recap: We find a creepy underground vault full of erased wielders, Aiden's name gets auto-added to the 'Congratulations, You Don't Exist Anymore' list, and then Cassius gives us something?"

Sarah frowned. "That's the part that doesn't make sense. If the Order wants to keep secrets, why give us anything at all?"

Aiden exhaled. "We're about to find out."

He hesitated, then followed his gut; the Codex's cover was already humming faintly in his hands, as if it recognized the shard. Aiden pressed the data chip against the etched margin of the pages, hoping it might respond.

For a moment, nothing happened.

Then—

The Codex reacted violently.

Its pages flipped on their own, the ink shifting, realigning into something new.

"Every Wielder Walks a Path of Their Own Making. But The Path is Never Free of Shadows."

The display flickered, and suddenly, a projection of Cassius appeared in front of them, his image slightly grainy, but clear enough to see his unwavering gaze.

"If you are seeing this, Aiden Cross, then you have ignored my warning."

Aiden's --. "Yeah, that sounds about right."

Cassius's projection continued, as if anticipating his response.

"I imagine you believe we are your enemies. That we wish to stop you from learning the truth. That is not entirely incorrect."

Kyle scoffed. "Wow. Great sales pitch, buddy."

"But consider this. If the Order was as ruthless as you assume, you would not be alive to hear this message."

Sarah folded her arms. "He's got a point."

Cassius's gaze hardened, his voice lowering.

"We have spent centuries ensuring that history remains stable. That the mistakes of past wielders do not repeat themselves.

The Primordial Sect would have you believe that breaking the Seals will restore what was lost. They are wrong. It will only destroy what remains."

Blu's ears twitched, his gaze darkening. "He's lying."

Aiden frowned. "Maybe. Maybe not."

Cassius paused, as if choosing his next words carefully.

"But if you refuse to listen to me, then at least listen to yourself. You have already begun questioning the nature of your power, haven't you?"

Aiden stiffened.

Because Cassius was right.

The Destiny Gun had not reacted predictably to the artifacts they had found. It had not simply fired, destroyed, or restored. It had responded to something deeper—his own uncertainty.

Cassius's voice lowered.

"The gun does not choose. It follows. And if you do not know what you are fighting for, it will shape history in ways you cannot control."

Aiden's grip on the Codex tightened.

Sarah exhaled. "Okay, so what exactly is he offering?"

As if on cue, Cassius's projection glitched slightly, before stabilizing again.

"I am giving you one opportunity to leave this path behind."

A map appeared beside him, displaying a set of coordinates.

"This location will take you beyond the influence of the Nexus. You can disappear before the Cycle consumes you."

Mark squinted at the floating map. "Those coordinates are miles from any recorded ley line. It's basically the middle of nowhere."

Silence filled the room.

Kyle blinked. "Wait. Did he just offer you witness protection from reality itself?"

Mark studied the map. "The coordinates… they're nowhere near any ley lines or Nexus points. If this is real, the Order is offering you a way to escape whatever's coming next."

Sarah crossed her arms. "Yeah. Because they're afraid of what happens if he keeps going."

Blu turned to Aiden. "You're not considering it, are you?"

Aiden's stomach twisted.

A part of him wanted to dismiss it outright. To tell himself that this was just another manipulation tactic from the Order.

But another part of him—the part that had felt the weight of the Destiny Gun since the moment he first held it—wondered if Cassius was right.

The gun was shaping reality based on him.

And if he made the wrong choice…

Would he even know it?

*****

Aiden exhaled, stepping away from the projection. "Cassius is afraid of something."

Sarah nodded. "Yeah. You."

Kyle frowned. "So… what's the plan? Do we pretend we never saw this and keep going?"

Mark hesitated. "Actually… we should consider it."

Everyone turned to him.

Mark adjusted his glasses, uncomfortable under their stares. "I'm not saying we take the offer. But we do need to consider why they're willing to give Aiden an out. The Order doesn't just erase wielders. They erase the ones who go too far."

Aiden looked back at the projection. Cassius had said one last thing before the recording ended.

"You will have one chance to walk away before it's too late. I suggest you take it."

Blu's voice was steady. "Then we don't give them what they want."

Aiden met his gaze.

Kyle sighed. "Well, there goes our chance to live peacefully in the middle of nowhere."

Sarah smirked. "You would've been bored within a week."

Kyle grinned. "Okay, that's fair."

Aiden turned back to the Codex, watching as the last words of the projection burned themselves into the page.

"The gun does not choose. It follows."

His hand hovered over the book's surface.

Cassius had offered him a way out.

But the thought of abandoning everyone who'd already been erased—everyone whose names he'd just seen—made his stomach twist. He wasn't ready to walk away.

Aiden shuts the Codex, turning to the others.

"We're going to find the Dagger of Nexus."

Sarah raised an eyebrow. "Even though the Order says it's too dangerous?"

Aiden smirked. "Especially because of that."

The Codex pulsed in response, as if acknowledging his resolve.

And for the first time since this began—

Aiden felt certain about what came next.

The Primordial Sect

Location: Hidden Exhibit Chamber – Atlantean Relics Section

The convention's lower levels were quiet—too quiet.

Aiden and his team moved carefully through the restricted exhibit space, following a lead from the Codex's most recent update.

Sarah tapped a panel on the wall, scanning the holographic directory. "Okay. According to this, the oldest relics in the convention center are in this wing—stuff recovered from deep-sea expeditions."

Mark adjusted his glasses. "And if Cassius wasn't lying, then the Order has already tried to bury whatever we're about to find."

Kyle grinned. "Which means it's definitely worth seeing."

Blu, however, was tense. His golden eyes darted around the dimly lit hallways, his ears twitching. "Something's off."

Aiden frowned. "What do you mean?"

Blu inhaled sharply. "The air feels… unstable. Like something is shifting."

Mark paled. "That sounds like a Nexus disruption."

Kyle groaned. "Great. Reality-breaking nonsense incoming."

Sarah motioned them forward. "Whatever it is, we deal with it. Let's go."

Aiden pushed open the large double doors, stepping inside the Atlantean Relics Exhibit.

And the moment they did—

Everything changed.

Location: The Atlantean Exhibit – A Shift in Reality

The room was massive, lined with glass cases filled with artifacts, illuminated in soft blue lighting. The air smelled faintly of salt water, despite them being miles from any ocean.

Aiden immediately noticed the strange murals on the walls—depictions of warriors holding weapons that looked like the Destiny Gun... but different.

Mark frowned, studying one of the inscriptions. "These engravings... they predate every known civilization. They shouldn't exist."

Kyle, reading another plaque, raised an eyebrow. "'The Last Wielder Who Reached the First Seal Never Returned.' That's comforting."

Sarah pointed at the center of the room, where a massive stone pedestal held a broken relic.

Aiden stepped closer.

It was a shattered stone tablet, its surface cracked but still etched with symbols.

Blu stiffened immediately. "That symbol—"

The engraving was a dagger piercing through a ring of stars.

Mark's voice was barely a whisper. "The Dagger of Nexus."

*****

Aiden reached for the artifact—

But before his fingers could touch it, the entire room darkened.

The lights flickered, shadows stretching unnaturally across the walls.

Blu growled. "They're here."

Sarah spun around. "Who's—"

A figure stepped from the darkness, clad in deep emerald and gold robes, their face hidden behind a ceremonial mask.

Kyle let out an exaggerated sigh. "Oh great. Cultists. Fantastic."

The masked figure's voice was calm, but commanding.

"You are meddling in forces you do not understand, Wielder.

"We have watched you ever since you opened the ledger the Order tried to bury."

More figures emerged from the shadows, all wearing the same dark robes, marked with ancient sigils.

Mark swallowed. "The Primordial Sect."

Aiden squared his shoulders. "You people have been rewriting history just as much as the Order has."

The leader tilted their head. "No. We seek to correct history, not erase it."

They stepped forward, gesturing toward the broken tablet.

"This is a fragment of what once was—a time before the Order tampered with the Nexus. Before they sealed away the truth."

Blu's claws flexed. "You mean before they stopped you from destroying everything?"

The leader laughed softly. "Ah. The Guardian speaks. How amusing."

Aiden stepped in front of Blu, his grip tightening on the Destiny Gun. "What do you want?"

The leader paused, then extended a hand.

"Join us."

Silence.

Sarah's brows shot up. "That's… a bold offer."

The leader nodded. "You have seen the ledger. You now know the truth —that wielders do not die. They are erased. And what better way to ensure you are not the next name crossed from history than to stand with those who fight against the cycle?"

Aiden felt the gun pulse at his side.

His mind flashed to Phelipandro's words.

"I failed because I trusted it. Will you do the same?"

Aiden's --. "You think I'll just trust you over the Order?"

The leader's tone was calm, but firm. "The Order protects a lie. We seek to break free of it."

Then—

"The only way to undo what has been lost is to break the next Seal."

*****

Blu snarled. "That's not happening."

The leader sighed. "Then we have no choice."

In an instant, the air warped, and reality itself flickered like a broken signal.

The Sect moved with unnatural speed, attacking with energy-based weapons that shimmered like mirages.

Aiden dodged, pulling the Destiny Gun just in time to counter a bolt of energy.

Sarah and Kyle moved fast—Kyle using his tech disruptor to knock an attacker off balance, while Sarah engaged in hand-to-hand combat, blocking strikes with precision.

Mark ducked behind a display, rapidly typing on his tablet. "If I can overload the exhibit's energy field, I might be able to destabilize their connection to the Nexus!"

Blu lunged at one of the robed figures, claws flashing, forcing them back.

Aiden fired a shot—not at the Sect, but at the ceiling, shattering a light fixture and plunging part of the room into shadows.

The Destiny Gun's blast was different this time.

The energy distorted—not just firing a projectile, but bending the space where it struck.

The leader's eyes widened beneath their mask.

"You… you are already altering reality."

Aiden's breath hitched. The gun was responding to him more than ever before.

Sarah took down another opponent, panting. "Okay, is it just me, or does the gun feel… unstable?"

Blu, knocking an enemy unconscious, shook his head. "Not unstable. Focused."

The leader held up a hand, signaling their forces to stop.

"Enough. This battle does not serve us."

Aiden didn't lower his weapon. "You tried to kill us."

The leader chuckled. "If we wanted you dead, Wielder, you would be."

They gestured to the broken relic.

"Take the fragment. Seek the truth of the Dagger. But know this—when the time comes, you will have to decide whether to wield the past… or break free of it."

With a final pulse of energy, the Primordial Sect vanished, leaving the exhibit in eerie silence.

Aiden exhaled slowly, lowering the gun.

Kyle dusted himself off. "Soooo. That was a thing."

Mark hurried forward, examining the shattered tablet. "They wanted us to find this."

Sarah crossed her arms. "That means whatever it says… is something the Order doesn't want us to know."

Aiden picked up the fragment. The engraving of the Dagger piercing the ring of stars was clear.

Blu's voice was barely above a whisper. "I've seen this before."

Sarah turned. "What?"

Blu's golden eyes flickered with something unsettling.

"Not in this time. But in another."

Aiden's pulse quickened.

For the first time, they weren't just chasing answers.

They were holding a piece of lost history in their hands.

The Dagger of Nexus Vision
Location: Hidden Exhibit Chamber –
Atlantean Relics Section

Aiden held the fragment of the broken tablet in his hands, the engraved image of a dagger piercing a ring of stars standing out against the cracked stone surface.

His fingers traced the edges, his mind buzzing with questions.

Blu stood still, his golden eyes locked onto the artifact. His breath came slowly, controlled, but Aiden could see it—the subtle tremble in his hands.

Sarah shifted uncomfortably. "Blu. What did you mean before? That you've seen this before?"

Blu exhaled slowly. "Not here. Not now. But... somewhere. Somewhen."

Aiden's grip on the artifact tightened.

The past wasn't just forgotten. It was sealed.

The Codex reacted, its pages flipping wildly on its own.

Golden light bled from the tablet's engraving into the open pages, thin threads of energy stitching stone and parchment together.

And then—Aiden's vision fractured.

Aiden's Vision – The Forgotten Wielder

Darkness.

Then—a pulse of light.

Aiden found himself standing at the edge of a vast ocean, the sky above him unnaturally clear, as if the very air shimmered with unseen forces.

In the distance, a towering stone archway stood against the horizon, its ancient symbols glowing faintly.

Then, he saw him.

A lone figure stood at the center of the arch, clad in black and gold robes, the fabric billowing slightly from an unseen wind.

His hands held something—a dagger, its blade humming with an unnatural golden aura.

Aiden tried to step forward, but his body didn't respond.

The man turned his head slightly, as if sensing him.

His voice was deep, layered, as if speaking from multiple points in time.

"You shouldn't be here yet, Aiden."

Aiden's breath caught. "Who are you?"

The man sighed, shaking his head slightly. "You already know."

The answer hit Aiden like a wave of static.

Phelipandro.

Aiden -expression. "If you're really Phelipandro, then tell me—what happened to you? What happened to the other wielders?"

Phelipandro turned fully now, revealing golden tattoos etched into his skin, pulsing in rhythm with the Nexus energy around him.

He lifted the dagger.

The blade shifted, its shape unstable, flickering between different forms—a sword, a spear, a staff—before settling back into a dagger.

"This is the choice you don't know you have to make yet."

Aiden took a shaky breath. "What does that mean?"

Phelipandro's expression hardened.

"The Destiny Gun doesn't rewrite history, Aiden. It preserves it."

Aiden felt the words sink into his bones. "Then what does the Dagger do?"

Phelipandro exhaled.

"It erases it."

The weight of the revelation hit like a shockwave.

Aiden's heart pounded. "You mean—"

Phelipandro stepped forward, closing the distance between them in an instant. His golden eyes burned like fire.

"The reason the Order buried the Dagger… is because it doesn't just undo history. "It severs it completely."

The Breaking Point

Aiden staggered backward, but his body remained trapped within the vision, unable to wake up.

Phelipandro studied him, his voice quieter now. "I thought I could fix everything once. I thought I could undo the mistakes made before me."

He turned the dagger over in his hands.

"But wielding the Dagger means making a choice. And no wielder before you has had the strength to make it."

Aiden swallowed hard. "What choice?"

Phelipandro's gaze locked onto his.

"Do you want to change history, Aiden? Or do you want to erase it?"

Aiden's pulse pounded in his ears. "That's not a choice. That's—"

Phelipandro lifted his free hand, and suddenly—

Aiden was standing in a different time.

The ocean was gone.

He was in a massive ruined city, the ground cracked with energy, the sky above split between two colliding timelines.

A single figure stood at the heart of it all, wearing armor lined with ancient engravings.

And in their hand—

The Destiny Gun.

Aiden's breath caught. "Who is that?"

Phelipandro's voice was almost mournful.

"The last wielder who tried to break the cycle."

The figure raised the gun—and reality itself began collapsing around them.

The ground fractured, entire buildings dissolving into nothingness.

Aiden's chest tightened. "This—this is what happens if I make the wrong choice?"

Phelipandro didn't answer.

Because he didn't need to.

The vision collapsed—

And Aiden woke up gasping for breath.

Back in the Present – The Exhibit

Blu was crouched beside him, his hands gripping Aiden's shoulders. "Breathe."

Aiden gasped, his entire body shaking. His mind was still reeling from the vision—the city, the collapsing timelines, the truth about the Dagger.

Sarah knelt beside him. "What happened? You just collapsed."

Aiden looked down at the fragment of the broken tablet still in his hands.

The engraving of the dagger piercing the ring of stars was clearer now.

Like it had been waiting for him to remember.

Kyle helped Aiden sit up. "I'm guessing from the way you look like you just saw a ghost, you had a fun trip to time-travel hell?"

Aiden exhaled. "Not time travel. A warning."

Sarah frowned. "From who?"

Aiden hesitated, then spoke the name out loud.

"Phelipandro."

Blu tensed.

Mark rubbed the back of his head. "Okay, that's great and all, but what specifically did he say?"

Aiden's fingers curled around the tablet fragment.

His voice was quiet, but heavy.

"The Destiny Gun doesn't rewrite history.
"It preserves it."

Sarah narrowed her eyes. "Then what does the Dagger do?"

Aiden swallowed.

"It erases it completely."

Silence.

Kyle broke it first. "Soooo, just for clarification—if we find the Dagger, are we looking at potential timeline deletion on a scale of 'bad' or 'apocalypse'?"

Aiden ran a hand through his hair, still catching his breath.

"If Phelipandro was telling the truth… then the Order didn't just hide the Dagger because it was dangerous."

He met Blu's gaze.

"They hid it because it was the only thing that could stop the cycle from repeating."

Blu exhaled sharply, looking away.

Aiden took a deep breath, his mind finally clearing.

The Order wanted him to turn back.

The Primordial Sect wanted him to break the Seals.

But Phelipandro had shown him the real choice.

Rewrite history. Or erase it completely.

The Forgotten Wielder: Phelipandro's Eternal Cycle

Later that night, back in the team's cramped hotel room near the convention center, Sarah sat at the little desk, her fingers tracing the edges of the brittle parchment before her. The letter had arrived minutes ago, slid under their door without explanation, sealed with a crest she had only seen once before—the sigil of the Primordial Sect. The date at the top? February 14th, 1925. A century ago.

Her breath caught as she unfolded the letter.

"To the one who seeks the truth,

Know this: The one you call Phelipandro was not always as you see him now. Before the fracture, before the Order's betrayal, he was not a man. He was a Nexus Entity, a guardian of the cosmic weave, neither mortal nor bound to time. He watched over the ley lines as one might watch the stars—existing beyond them, shaping the flow of existence without ever truly touching it.

But when the fracture began, and the Order shattered the balance, the impossible occurred. The ley lines, once untouchable, were torn apart. Phelipandro's essence was ensnared in the chaos. The Order, hungry for control, captured his Nexus form, seeking to weaponize his knowledge. To escape their grasp, his consciousness did the only thing it could—it fled.

But where does a being of pure existence go when there is no longer a home to return to?

Into the shell of a man.

His mind found an anchor in the fractured world—a mortal vessel, forged from the remnants of broken realities. And so, Phelipandro became a Wielder of the Destiny Gun, not by choice, but by necessity. For centuries, he worked to restore balance, walking the path of mortals while the Order held his true self prisoner.

Yet even as a Wielder, he was not safe. The Order sought to reclaim what had escaped them. They sent one of their own—an infiltrator, hidden within the Primordial Sect. This traitor gained Phelipandro's trust, learning his weaknesses, waiting for the moment to strike.

And when that moment came, they did not kill him. No... they did worse.

They took the Gun.

And with it, they erased him from history.

But some things do not vanish so easily.

A Nexus cannot be destroyed, only displaced. And so Phelipandro became an echo, his mortal identity erased, his memories shattered, his existence reduced to fragments drifting through the weave of fractured realities. He no longer remembers who he was, only that he is searching for something... for someone.

Himself.

One day, he will find his truth. When that day comes, the weave shall tremble once more, and the echoes of what was lost shall call out to the one who was forgotten. Until then, watch the ley lines.

He is still out there.

Still searching.

Signed,
A Keeper of the Lost Thread"

Sarah's hands trembled as she lowered the letter.

A hundred years ago, someone knew this would happen. Someone knew that Phelipandro's cycle was not yet finished.

She turned to the others, her voice barely a whisper.

"He's still out there."

And for the first time, she understood: Phelipandro wasn't just a lost wielder. He was a living echo of the ley lines themselves, forever bouncing between realities, forever searching for the one thing stolen from him—his own identity.

If they could find him before the Order did…

Maybe they could restore him. Maybe they could break the cycle.

Maybe, just maybe… he could finally become whole.

CHAPTER 12: THE BRIDGE

Echoes of the Forgotten
Location: Aiden's Apartment –
Late Night, Hours After the Encounter with the Order

The digital clock on Aiden's nightstand blinked 3:42 AM.

Outside, the city was quiet, bathed in a soft haze of neon glow from the distant skyline. The usual hum of traffic and murmuring nightlife was strangely absent, as if the world had momentarily stilled.

Aiden sat on the edge of his bed, unable to sleep.

The events of the last day churned in his mind—the Codex rewriting itself, the Order offering him a way out, the Primordial Sect attacking them in the relic exhibit, and Blu's cryptic words:

"Not in this time. But in another."

This wasn't just about surviving Comic-Con anymore. Someone was pruning reality—erasing wielders, sealing away weapons—and the next Seal was sitting somewhere at the center of it all, waiting for him to choose wrong.

His grip tightened on the Codex resting on his lap. Its cover was warm, almost pulsing, as if the book itself had something more to say.

But it remained closed, its pages still and silent.

Aiden sighed and ran a hand over his face. Fatigue weighed on him, but his mind refused to rest.

He exhaled sharply and lay back against his pillow, staring at the ceiling.

That was when the whispering began.

A Memory That Shouldn't Exist

At first, it was faint—just a ripple in the air, like a conversation drifting through a half-opened door in time.

Then—a voice.

"Do not look for me."

Aiden sat up immediately, his heart hammering.

The room had shifted.

Objects weren't quite where they had been—his desk lamp was slightly off-center, the jacket he had tossed on the chair was now folded neatly, and his reflection in the window...

Wasn't moving.

Aiden's breath hitched. His reflection stood frozen, staring straight ahead, unmoving despite his rapid breathing.

Then—it blinked.

A rush of images flooded his mind.

*****

He was no longer in his room.

He stood in a vast, ruined hall, its pillars cracked, its ceiling partially collapsed, letting in thin streaks of moonlight through the jagged gaps.

A man stood ahead of him, cloaked in shadows, back turned.

Aiden tried to speak, but no sound came out.

The man lifted his head slightly, sensing Aiden's presence.

In his right hand, he held the Destiny Gun.

But something was wrong.

The gun's usual intricate engravings were missing, its form distorted, as if it were unfinished or incomplete.

The man's voice was a whisper stretched across time.

"This is what happens when the Seals remain closed."

Aiden felt a deep ache in his chest, an overwhelming sense of loss that wasn't his own.

The man finally turned—

But he had no face.

Just a blank void, where his features should have been.

It wasn't emptiness—it was absence, like the space where a name had been scraped off a gravestone.

Aiden stumbled backward.

The whisper returned, clearer this time.

"Forgotten. Erased. Do not become one of us."

The world collapsed into darkness.

Aiden gasped awake, sitting upright so fast he nearly fell off the bed.

His pulse pounded against his ribs, his breath coming in short bursts.

The Codex lay open beside him—but he hadn't opened it.

And on the page in front of him—

"Do not look for me."

If the erased were telling him to stop, what did that say about the people trying to keep them buried?

Blu stood in the doorway, his golden eyes sharp, alert. "It happened, didn't it?"

Aiden swallowed hard. "You knew this was coming."

Blu crossed his arms. "I suspected." He hesitated. "You saw one of them, didn't you?"

Aiden -expression. "Not just any wielder. One that was erased completely."

Blu exhaled sharply and sat on the windowsill, tail flicking in agitation. "That's what happens when the Seals remain unbroken for too long."

Aiden's gaze snapped to him. "You've seen this before."

Blu hesitated, then nodded. "Not personally. But I remember stories."

"Guardians used to whisper about wielders who outlived their own timelines—bodies still walking, but no one left who remembered their names."

Sarah's voice came from the hallway, groggy but serious. "If you two are going to have a dramatic cryptic conversation at four in the morning, can you at least clue the rest of us in?"

She and Kyle stood in the doorway, Kyle rubbing his eyes. "Dude, if you're gonna be haunted, do it at normal hours."

Aiden ran a hand through his hair. "I saw someone. A past wielder. Or what was left of them."

Mark, now awake and standing in the hall, frowned. "What do you mean, left of them?"

Aiden exhaled, steadying himself.

"They weren't just forgotten. They were erased from existence."

The room fell silent.

Kyle scratched the back of his head. "Okay. That's bad."

Sarah sighed. "Understatement of the century."

Blu finally spoke. "This is why you can't use the gun carelessly."

Aiden narrowed his eyes. "I haven't."

Blu shook his head. "Not yet. But the more you uncover the past, the more unstable your own existence becomes. That's why you saw him."

Aiden stared at the words in the Codex again.

"Do not look for me."

e swallowed hard. "It's too late for that."

Blu studied him carefully. "You're sure?"

Aiden met his gaze.

"If I don't find out what happened to them, then I'll be next."

Location: Abandoned Train Yard – 4:58 AM

The early morning air was cold and thick with fog, the distant hum of the city muffled beneath the weight of an eerie silence.

Aiden walked ahead, his boots crunching softly on the gravel as he followed a trail of flickering streetlights—the only sign that he was going the right way.

Behind him, Blu and Sarah kept pace, while Kyle and Mark trailed a few steps behind, yawning from the lack of sleep.

Kyle rubbed his arms. "Okay, not to sound ungrateful or anything, but are we sure this isn't an elaborate prank to get us mugged by a time-traveling ghost?"

Sarah sighed. "No, Kyle. Pecos wouldn't bother with theatrics. If he wanted to mess with us, he'd just make reality fold in on itself again."

Kyle blinked. "Oh, good. That's so much more comforting."

Aiden exhaled sharply, gripping the Destiny Gun at his side.

Pecos had left a message in the Codex after Aiden's vision.

"Meet me where history stands still."

It hadn't taken long to decode the meaning—the abandoned train yard, where a ley line rupture had once frozen a single locomotive in time, leaving it untouched by decay for over eighty years.

Sarah looked around as they walked deeper into the railyard. "I still don't get why Pecos couldn't just appear in my kitchen like last time."

Blu flicked his tail. "Because this is a test."

Aiden frowned. "A test for what?"

Blu exhaled. "To see if you understand what the gun really is."

Before Aiden could ask what that meant—

A low whistle cut through the air.

They all turned toward the tracks.

There, standing atop an old rusted cargo container, hands in his coat pockets, was Pecos.

His silver hair was messy, as usual, his boots scuffed from years of travel, but his mischievous grin was as sharp as ever.

"Well, well. Looks like you kids didn't get lost after all."

Pecos hopped down gracefully, landing in front of them without a sound.

His gaze landed on Aiden, eyes filled with knowing amusement. "You've been busy, Wielder."

Aiden folded his arms. "You knew about the erased wielders."

Pecos nodded. "Of course I did."

Sarah scowled. "And you didn't think to warn us?"

Pecos gave her an easy shrug. "Would you have believed me if I had?"

Sarah opened her mouth—then stopped, frowning.

Kyle pointed at her. "That's fair. You would've called him a cryptic liar and ignored him."

Pecos smirked. "See? I know my audience."

Aiden sighed. "Alright. We're here. What's this test?"

Pecos studied him for a long moment, then motioned to the empty train tracks.

"See that?" he asked.

Aiden turned his head. At the center of the yard stood a train frozen mid-motion, its wheels hovering inches above the rails, as if reality itself had simply stopped moving around it.

Kyle whistled. "That is… deeply unsettling."

Pecos crossed his arms. "That train's been stuck there since 1941. When the ley lines shifted, time stopped around it."

Sarah frowned. "We already know that. What does it have to do with Aiden's test?"

Pecos smirked. "Simple. Fix it."

Aiden stiffened. "What?"

Pecos tapped the gun at Aiden's side. "That thing in your hand? The Destiny Gun doesn't just erase. It preserves. It chooses."

Aiden clenched his jaw. "You're saying I can restart time for the train."

Pecos nodded. "If you're the right kind of Wielder."

Aiden turned back toward the train.

The Destiny Gun pulsed against his side, as if responding to his growing focus.

Sarah crossed her arms. "What happens if he fires?"

Pecos tilted his head. "Depends. If Aiden does it right, time starts moving again, and that train finishes a journey it never got to complete."

Kyle shifted. "And if he does it wrong?"

Pecos smiled lazily. "Well, let's hope he doesn't erase the concept of rail travel from history."

Mark tensed. "That's not funny."

Aiden exhaled slowly, stepping toward the tracks.

He raised the Destiny Gun, letting its energy build.

The air around him shifted, humming with potential.

But something inside him hesitated.

"Every Wielder Walks a Path of Their Own Making. But The Path is Never Free of Shadows."

Cassius's words echoed in his mind.

Aiden frowned, lowering the gun slightly.

Pecos raised an eyebrow. "Problem?"

Aiden turned to him. "You're not testing whether I can restart time."

Pecos's smirk widened slightly. "No. I'm testing whether you think before you shoot."

Aiden's fingers tightened around the gun.

Then, he closed his eyes.

He let himself feel the space around him—the subtle energy shifts, the stillness of time, the faint tremor of something buried in the ley lines.

And that's when he felt it.

The train wasn't just frozen in time.

It was trapped inside a choice.

Someone—long ago—had used the gun here before.

Aiden's breath caught. If he fired now, he wouldn't just restart time. He'd be undoing whatever decision had been made here before him.

"Do not look for me."

The faceless wielder's whisper from his vision returned, louder this time.

Aiden's grip on the gun tightened.

Then—he lowered it.

Sarah blinked. "Aiden?"

Aiden exhaled. "This isn't my choice to undo."

Pecos grinned. "Good answer."

With a snap of his fingers, the train disappeared.

The entire yard shuddered, reality correcting itself in an instant.

Kyle took a stumbling step back, wide-eyed. "Okay—what the hell just happened?"

Pecos gave a carefree shrug. "I needed to know if Aiden understands the weight of that thing in his hands. And now I do."

For the first time, Aiden realized the test hadn't been about power at all. It had been about restraint.

Sarah crossed her arms. "And what did you learn?"

Pecos smirked. "That he's not an idiot."

Aiden exhaled, still processing what he'd just felt. "That train wasn't just frozen in time. Someone made a choice to leave it there."

Pecos gave him a knowing nod. "And the moment you fire that gun at something, you take responsibility for every choice made before you."

Aiden swallowed hard.

Kyle pointed at Pecos. "Okay, but be honest—if Aiden had fired, what would've actually happened?"

Pecos shrugged. "Dunno. Probably something catastrophic. Or maybe just a loud noise. Who's to say?"

Kyle groaned. "I hate this guy."

Sarah sighed. "Welcome to my world."

Aiden turned to Pecos. "You have something for me, don't you?"

Pecos grinned. "Oh, you're finally learning how this works."

He pulled something from his coat—a fragment of a map, its edges burned but its markings still clear.

Aiden took it carefully, scanning the text.

Mark adjusted his glasses. "Where does it lead?"

Aiden's pulse quickened.

"A lost city beneath a modern one."

He pictured skyscrapers sitting on top of drowned streets, whole neighborhoods ghosted beneath the foundations of the present—a city stacked on its own grave.

Blu's tail flicked. "The next Seal."

Pecos stretched. "Better hurry. The Order and the Sect won't be far behind."

"The Vanishing Name"
Location: Sarah and Kyle's Research Space –
Early Morning, 6:30 AM

The sun had just begun cresting the horizon, casting a dim golden glow through the large windows of Sarah's makeshift research space—a converted loft-style office filled with piles of old books, digital screens, and half-drunk coffee cups.

Aiden, Sarah, Kyle, and Mark had returned after Pecos's test, determined to piece together the mystery surrounding the erased wielders and the location of the next Nexus Seal.

The atmosphere was tense but focused. Blu sat near the window, alert but silent. Sobacco had faded from visibility, likely recharging somewhere in Aiden's subconscious.

Sarah sat cross-legged on the floor, spreading out several aged documents they had recovered from the underground ledger of wielders.

Kyle leaned over her shoulder. "So, what exactly are we looking for again? Secret coded messages? Hidden treasure maps? A note that says 'This Way to the Super Apocalypse'?"

Sarah didn't look up. "We're looking for a pattern. Something the Order missed when they erased the past wielders."

Aiden exhaled and leaned against the nearest table, arms crossed. "If we can find something the ley lines haven't erased, we might get an actual lead instead of following the Codex's riddles."

Mark, typing rapidly on his tablet, adjusted his glasses. "I've been running cross-references on every name we've found so far. The problem is that the official archives don't list them. It's like they never existed."

Aiden frowned. "Not even a birth record?"

Mark shook his head. "Nope. It's like someone went back and rewrote history to exclude them entirely."

Blu finally spoke. "That's exactly what happened."

They turned to him.

His golden eyes were unreadable. "You need to understand—the Order doesn't just erase people. They erase the consequences of their existence. The Nexus doesn't tolerate instability. If a wielder disrupts the balance, they are unmade."

Kyle whistled lowly. "That's gotta be the single most horrifying thing I've heard today. And I was just almost responsible for deleting an entire train from reality, so that's saying something."

Aiden ignored Kyle's sarcasm, his fingers clenching slightly. The weight of Blu's words settled uncomfortably.

If a wielder was erased, then—how many people had simply disappeared from history without anyone remembering them?

Sarah narrowed her eyes at the documents. "Alright. If the Order erased their existence, then let's look for what's missing. The gaps. Maybe history doesn't remember them, but it sure as hell will remember the empty spaces where they should have been."

She pulled a long strip of parchment from the pile and unrolled it.

Aiden leaned over her shoulder, scanning the handwritten records of past wielders. The list ran in chronological order—each name neatly inscribed in ancient ink.

But there was a gap.

A noticeable blank space between two recorded wielders, as if someone had purposefully removed a name.

Sarah tapped the gap. "There."

Kyle frowned. "Isn't that just a formatting issue?"

Mark shook his head. "No. The spacing isn't random. This was deliberate."

Aiden's pulse quickened. He reached for the Codex, flipping to the pages where the ledger of wielders had appeared before.

The text shifted—realigning itself, revealing a faded, barely legible name where there had been none before.

Aiden froze.

Sarah's breath caught. "Wait… it's coming back?"

Kyle stepped forward. "But I thought the erased names were gone permanently?"

Mark adjusted his glasses. "Not permanently. Not if the Order only covered up the gaps instead of fully deleting them."

Blu stood abruptly. His voice was calm but sharp. "Don't touch it."

Aiden's fingers halted just inches from the page.

Kyle raised an eyebrow. "Uh, is the book gonna explode or something?"

Blu's tail flicked. "No. But if Aiden interacts with it, he might replace the missing name with his own."

Silence.

Aiden stiffened.

Sarah swore under her breath. "The Codex is rewriting history in real-time."

Aiden exhaled slowly, pulling his hand back.

If he touched the page, would he be filling the void?
Would he become the next name erased from time?

Blu's gaze didn't waver. "This is how it happens. This is why past wielders vanish. Because they follow the wrong path, and history rewrites itself to correct their existence."

"That's how the Cycle survives," Blu said. "It doesn't delete the story. It swaps in a new victim."

Kyle muttered. "Okay, that's beyond messed up."

Aiden's mind raced.

If the Codex was revealing the erased names now, it meant something was weakening the Order's control.

And that meant…

Someone had undone the first piece of the Order's deception.

Sarah suddenly gasped. "Aiden—look at this!"

She pointed to a secondary document, one that should have listed records of historical events surrounding each wielder's time period.

But instead of listing events, one name was missing.

Aiden leaned in—his stomach tightening.

The missing name wasn't from the Codex.

It was from an entirely different book.

Sarah's voice was barely above a whisper. "This name didn't just vanish from the wielders' record. It was removed from history itself."

Kyle blinked. "Wait, how is that even possible?"

Mark ran a quick scan on the parchment with his tablet. "If my guess is right—this record was altered manually. Someone didn't just use ley lines to erase it. They physically removed this information from multiple sources."

Blu's ears flattened. "Which means someone—right now—is actively trying to stop you from uncovering the truth."

Aiden stared at the name on the page.

It was faint, barely visible, but it was there.

And it was changing before his eyes.

Aiden Cross.

The old ink didn't make room—it pushed something out, as if his name were being jammed into a space where another should have been.

Aiden's chest tightened.

Kyle swore. "Okay, I'm no expert, but I'm pretty sure your name wasn't supposed to be there."

Sarah's expression darkened. "Someone's replacing the erased wielders with new ones."

Blu's voice was low, urgent. "That means we're out of time."

Aiden -expression. The Order had warned him once.

"You are becoming part of the Cycle."

Sarah grabbed the parchment and rolled it up. "We need to get out of here. If the Order finds out we're uncovering this, they'll—"

The lights in the room flickered.

Blu's fur bristled. "They already know."

Aiden's stomach dropped.

Kyle backed toward the door. "Uh, guys? We're not alone."

Aiden turned toward the shadows at the edge of the room.

The air warped, twisting unnaturally.

From the darkness, a figure emerged, clad in silver robes, their face half-obscured by shifting light.

Aiden recognized the uniform instantly.

The Order of Destiny had arrived.

"A Door in the Past"
Location: Sarah and Kyle's Research Space –
The Order Arrives

The air thickened.

Aiden's fingers curled instinctively around the Destiny Gun, his pulse steady but alert.

Across the room, the silver-robed figure stepped forward, their face obscured by shifting light, an unnatural distortion warping their features.

Sarah edged backward, tucking the parchment scroll into her jacket. Kyle, standing beside her, tapped at his smartwatch, likely trying to send a distress ping to their off-grid network.

Blu moved into a defensive stance, his golden eyes glowing slightly. "We don't have time for this."

Aiden's mind raced. The Order had erased past wielders, buried them under rewritten history.

And now they were here to stop him from remembering.

The figure spoke, their voice calm yet carrying an undeniable weight of authority.

"You were warned, Wielder."

Aiden exhaled sharply. "Yeah? Well, I don't listen very well."

The Order agent remained still, watching him carefully.

"Put down the Codex. Leave the ledger. Walk away now, and you will not be lost."

Sarah snorted. "Wow, so reassuring. Just erase our brains a little and everything will be fine, huh?"

Mark muttered under his breath. "I knew we should've encrypted our findings."

The Order agent's shimmering form flickered slightly, as if the space they occupied wasn't entirely stable.

"You are tampering with history that must remain untouched. The Nexus preserves what must be preserved. It is not for you to decide."

Aiden -expression.

Not for me to decide?

His mind flashed back to Pecos's test. To the train frozen in time. To the choice that wasn't his to undo.

But this?

This was different.

The Order had already made their choice.
And Aiden wasn't about to let them make his.

Blu growled lowly. "We need to leave. Now."

Aiden nodded sharply. "Sarah—window exit. Mark, cover the files. Kyle—"

Kyle grabbed a nearby metal chair and hurled it at the Order agent. "See ya, time cops!"

The chair phased straight through them.

Kyle swore. "Oh, come on—"

The agent tilted their head slightly, as if amused. "Futile."

Sarah slammed a button on the wall, triggering the emergency exit protocol.

A metal panel slid open, revealing a service tunnel that led out of the research space and into the lower levels of the old city infrastructure.

Aiden fired the Destiny Gun—not at the agent, but at the ground near their feet.

The impact rippled through reality, distorting space just enough to disrupt whatever frequency they were using to stabilize themselves.

The agent's form flickered violently.

Aiden didn't wait to see if they recovered.

"Move!"

The team bolted through the exit, vanishing into the depths of the old city.

Location: Abandoned Subway Tunnels – Beneath the City

The air was cooler underground, thick with the scent of old concrete and rusting metal.

Their footsteps echoed as they ran through the forgotten subway tunnels, remnants of an abandoned transit system buried beneath the modern city.

Blu led the way, his ears flicking at every sound.

Mark clutched his tablet close to his chest, still processing what had just happened. "How did they even get in? This place isn't connected to any active networks!"

"They didn't follow cables," Blu said quietly. "They followed you. Every time the Codex rewrites itself, it leaves a trail."

Kyle, still breathless, muttered, "Maybe next time we should ward the building with, I don't know, anti-time-travel stickers or something."

Sarah, glancing behind them, spoke between sharp breaths. "Aiden, what the hell did you do back there?"

Aiden frowned. "The gun didn't just fire a shot. It altered something."

Blu glanced at him. "Yes. And that means the Nexus is going to push back."

Aiden's stomach twisted. "How bad?"

Blu's golden eyes flickered. "That depends. Do you like being erased from history?"

Aiden cursed under his breath.

Kyle groaned. "That's, like, the worst way to answer that question, man."

Sarah slowed as they reached a cross-section of tunnels, eyeing an ancient, corroded door set into the wall.

She pointed. "This is it."

Aiden frowned. "You're sure?"

Sarah nodded. "This tunnel predates the modern city. The map fragment Pecos gave us—it lines up with old transit plans. This is the door the Order tried to erase."

Blu stepped closer, inspecting the carvings. "These aren't just structural markings."

Aiden followed his gaze.

Etched into the metal were intricate symbols—similar to those on the Destiny Gun.

But in the center of the design, faintly visible beneath layers of grime, was an inscription.

Aiden stepped forward, brushing away dust to reveal faded words.

"Only the Forgotten May Enter."

If the door only opened for the forgotten, then crossing it meant stepping closer to becoming one of them.

Mark muttered, "Well. That's not ominous or anything."

Sarah pulled out her holographic scanner, attempting to analyze the text. "I can barely translate this. It's some weird mix of old dialects—maybe Atlantean?"

Kyle sighed. "Why is it always the lost civilizations with the creepy warnings?"

Aiden, however, wasn't listening.

Something about the inscription resonated within him.

His heartbeat slowed.

He could feel the gun pulsing faintly at his side, not in alarm—but in recognition.

Blu noticed. "You feel it, don't you?"

Aiden nodded slowly. "Yeah. This door… it's meant for me."

Kyle raised an eyebrow. "I'd like to formally request a second opinion on that conclusion."

Sarah frowned. "You think it's some kind of test?"

Blu's expression was unreadable. "More like a filter. If the Nexus is designed to erase people, then this place…"

"…is where the erased remain."

Silence.

Aiden's fingers grazed the metal of the door, and suddenly—

A rush of static filled his ears.

The tunnel darkened, shadows stretching unnaturally.

Faint whispers echoed from the other side of the doorway—familiar voices, distorted and distant.

Sarah took a step back. "Aiden..."

Aiden's breath hitched.

Because he recognized one of the voices.

A voice he had only heard in dreams.

"Aiden Cross... You are not the first."

He thought of the ledger's blank spaces, of the faceless man in his room, of a first Wielder the Codex refused to keep on the page.

Aiden's pulse spiked.

Kyle's voice cut in, uneasy. "Guys? I think we just knocked on the wrong door."

The ground beneath them rumbled.

The door unlocked itself.

Blu's tail flicked sharply. "Whatever's on the other side... it's been waiting for you."

Aiden swallowed hard.

"Then let's meet it."

He pushed the door open—

And stepped through.

Behind him, the world that still remembered his name flickered at the edges. Ahead, in the dark beyond the threshold, waited the ones who had already been erased—and the truth about whether a Wielder could save them without vanishing beside them.

AFTERWORD

If you're reading this, you've walked with Aiden farther than he ever expected to go.

When this volume opened, the world still believed its history was mostly stable. Artifacts were curiosities. Old books were just collectibles. A stranger's warning could be ignored if you closed the door hard enough.

By the time you reach this page, that illusion has cracked.

You've seen what the Destiny Gun really is: not a toy, not a weapon in the simple sense, but a lever wired into the ley lines themselves. You've watched the Codex respond—not as a passive record, but as something that remembers, and occasionally refuses to forget what others tried to erase. You've watched names blur at the edges, choices echo longer than they should, and factions step out of the shadows to argue over who gets to decide what "really" happened.

Most importantly, you've seen Aiden realize that he isn't just holding power. He's holding consequences.

Volume I is the part of the story where the questions outnumber the answers on purpose. Who placed the Seals, and what did they erase to do it? Why do some past wielders vanish from every record except the Codex? What, exactly, is Atlantis—a ruin, a myth, or a draft the world keeps trying to revise? And why do the Watchers care so much about one boy with a gun and a book?

Those questions are the bridge into Volume II.

In the next volume, the map widens and the floor drops out. The journey that has only approached Atlantis will step inside it. The Seals move from rumor and theory into lived danger. The Order of Destiny stops being a distant hand and becomes something Aiden can look in the eye. The quiet hints that someone has been choosing which futures survive will harden into a truth that's much harder to look away from.

The cost of a shot will climb. So will the cost of doing nothing.

You'll see more of the people who have chosen to stand near Aiden—by loyalty, by accident, or because the ley lines themselves seem to keep folding them together. Blu's connection to the weave will matter in ways even he hasn't admitted yet. Sobacco's existence—and the question of whether a "mistake" can claim their own fate—will grow sharper. The field notes you've glimpsed in the appendices will stop feeling theoretical and start reading like survival advice.

Most of all, the theme that haunts this volume—who gets to write the world, and at what price—will be pushed to its breaking point. Volume II doesn't promise easy answers. It promises sharper ones. The kind you can't unknow once you've seen them.

If Volume I is the moment Aiden realizes the story is already in motion, Volume II is where he learns that the ending everyone keeps warning him about is not fixed—not yet. There are still versions of the future unwritten. There are still pages that resist ink.

Thank you for giving this first half of Arc I your time, your imagination, and a space on your shelf. If you choose to follow Aiden, Blu, and the rest into Volume II, I can promise you this: the world you return to will not be the same one you left on page one.

Some histories fight back when you try to edit them.

We're not done testing how far they'll go.

With gratitude for reading,
Hector L. Bones